Alaskan Healing

An Alaskan Healing Novel

Lana Voynich

Cover design by Lori Gnahn.

ISBN: 0615689132
ISBN-13: 978-0615689135

Dedication

For my parents who instilled my love of books.
Thank you for teaching me nothing is impossible.

Acknowledgments

I'd like to thank Loree Lough and Darcia Helle for their guidance; Becki Stradtman, Patsy Herzog, Joya Fields and Elysabeth Eldering for their encouragement and suggestions; and, last but certainly not least, my husband for his patience and understanding while the characters in this novel took over my life.

Chapter One

Shawn Nilsen wrestled her duffel bag from the backseat of the taxi cab and dropped it on the ground while she hurried to zip her canvas work jacket against the cold. It had been years since she'd been in Alaska, and she'd forgotten how cold it was in October. The wind off the harbor made her eyes water as she yanked her knit hat down over her ears. She knew she would get used to the temperature in time.

With a feeling of uneasiness, she hoisted the bag and slung it over her shoulder while glancing around the pier where she stood. She had been here earlier in the day for an interview with the captain of a fishing boat. If it could even be called an interview. They'd exchanged names, and the captain had told her when the boat was leaving, and handed her a list of recommended gear and necessary supplies. Shawn had agreed and left to make sure she had all the required items. Now she had a job to do.

She straightened her back and walked down the dock, avoiding the crews as they loaded groceries and bait onto the fishing vessels. She was going to fish king crab, which she'd never done before. And she was going to do it with people she'd never met before. Her step faltered when she saw the hull of the boat she'd be spending the next two weeks on; *The KayLeigh*.

She made her way down the eighty-two foot boat. As one of the smaller boats in the harbor, *The KayLeigh* would catch less crab than the larger boats, but Shawn didn't mind. She wasn't here to make a fortune, like most of the greenhorns who came to Alaska for the commercial fishing season. She needed to escape Seattle for a while to gain some perspective on her life and, in her mind, Alaska was as good a place as any.

Nervous, yet excited, about what she had agreed to do, she stepped onboard and approached the two people crouched by a crab pot. Cap Richards, who had hired her that morning, straightened and clapped the other person on the shoulder as he spoke. "Drake, this is the new hand, Shawn. Shawn, Drake."

The other man flipped up his welding mask, revealing he was younger than Cap, and peered at Shawn. "Real funny, Dad," he said and returned to repairing the metal frame of the trap.

Cap ran his hand through his gray hair. "No joke. Shawn's our third hand for this trip."

"That," Drake said, jerking his shoulder toward Shawn, "is a woman."

Shawn was surprised by his response. She'd assumed the crew would give her grief due to her lack of experience but hadn't even considered discrimination based on her gender.

"What's your point?" Cap rubbed a hand over his face and appeared to be uncomfortable with, but not surprised at, Drake's response.

Drake stood and dropped his welding mask on the deck, revealing short blonde hair, damp with sweat. "Women don't belong on boats."

Shawn stepped forward and tipped her head back a few degrees to gaze up at him. "Excuse me?"

"Women aren't strong enough for crabbing," Drake stated as if he was sharing common knowledge.

"How do you know if I'm strong enough or not? You don't know anything about me."

"All I need to know is you're a woman and that's pretty clear. Ain't it?"

"And that means I'm not good enough to work with you?" Shawn blinked as Drake turned his back to her and moved away. She wasn't in the mood to put up with anyone's attitude today. Learning her fiancé cleaned out her savings account and eloped with her best friend eight days ago had eliminated Shawn's sense of humor.

Cap cleared his throat. "Drake doesn't like women on the boat."

"Really? I wouldn't have guessed." Shawn faced Cap. "This isn't a good idea. I don't want to cause problems with your crew. If they don't trust me, it could get nasty out there."

"He'll get over it," Cap replied before raising his voice. "What's the problem, son?"

Drake sneered at Shawn over his shoulder from where he was coiling a line. "She is. I'm not willing to risk my life by crewing with some chick who's worried she might break a nail."

"I can be as tough as I need to be." Shawn dropped her bag and propped her fists on her hips. She hadn't thought it would be easy, but this was worse than she'd anticipated. She wasn't sure she wanted to work with him, but she wasn't going to take his insults without defending herself.

"This is a crab boat, girlie. You have no idea how tough you need to be," Drake said as he faced her.

Shawn fought the urge to look to Cap for assistance. She knew Drake would consider it a sign of weakness if she expected the captain to fight her battles. She hid her relief when Cap spoke in a stern tone.

"You questioning my decision?" When Drake didn't meet his gaze, Cap said, "Your Uncle Mike vouched for her."

Shawn turned away. "I don't need this." She'd come here to work, not to fight for feminine equality. She had her own doubts whether she would be able to do the job but assumed Cap had confidence in her since he'd hired her.

Drake laughed. "You can't even talk to fishermen. What made you think you could work with us?"

Shawn clenched her fists and pivoted on the ball of her foot. "I can talk to fishermen. It's jerks like you I have a problem communicating with. Probably because of the difference in our IQs." She lowered her voice and leaned close enough to smell the cinnamon gum he was chewing. Even as she spoke, she knew she was overreacting, but she had no desire to rein herself in. She'd leave, but he'd know she was upset before she left.

"What would it take to change your mind concerning me? To convince you I'm tough enough? Should I recite my qualifications? Tell you I spent my last five hundred bucks to get here? Maybe you'd like to call Mike and ask him about my service record with the Coast Guard. What if I punch you? Would that prove anything?"

Drake smirked menacingly. "You wouldn't dare."

"Why not? Because I'll lose my spot on this boat? You've done your best to convince me and him," Shawn jerked her shoulder toward Cap and continued, "that I can't do the job. If I get fired for punching you, you won't have to deal with me, and I won't have to deal with your asinine attitude."

"No, I don't think you've got the balls to do it," Drake replied.

"It all comes back to that, doesn't it? Your whole problem with me is that I don't have balls, huh?"

Apparently confident he had proven his point, Drake nodded. "Yeah, I guess that's it."

"You're wrong," Shawn retorted and punched him in the jaw, furious he assumed he could insult her without consequence just because she wore a bra.

Drake staggered back half a step before catching his balance. With eyes flashing, he moved toward her. "You're lucky you're a woman. 'Cause otherwise I'd knock you on your ass for that."

"Give it a shot." Shawn stood her ground, cursing her temper. One swing from him would knock her down, if it didn't topple her over the rail into the water, which was barely above freezing. She knew he had every right to strike back, but she wasn't going to concede defeat. She figured the only reason he'd staggered was from the shock of her hitting him. He was more than large enough to absorb a blow from her.

Cap dropped his huge hands to their shoulders and stepped between them. "That's enough of your crap, kids." He faced Shawn. "I don't tolerate violence among my crew."

"I understand. Sorry to waste your time." Shawn reached for her gear.

As she lifted her pack, Cap spoke. "I didn't fire you."

Shawn turned in disbelief. Drake was staring at Cap with the same surprised expression she felt on her face.

"What?" Drake asked Cap.

"I'm letting it slide this time. You practically begged her to hit you, probably because you thought you knew how I'd react. And if you can forget she's a woman long enough to brawl with her, you can work with her." He slapped Drake on the back. "Show her the boat."

Drake narrowed his eyes and clamped his mouth shut.

"You hear me?" Cap nudged Drake with his elbow.

Drake's eyes moved from Shawn to Cap and he jerked his chin down a fraction of an inch.

"I'm not going to work with someone who thinks I'll get him killed," Shawn said.

"Damn it, girl. You're working on this boat. I don't have time to find another hand before we leave." Cap stormed up to the wheelhouse, slamming the door.

Shawn glowered at his back, wondering how the two men normally got along. The air was thick with tension and she didn't know how much of it was due to her presence and how much was standard.

If they usually got along great and the friction was entirely her fault, it would make for an unbearable trip. But on the other hand, if they always got along in this manner, she wasn't looking forward to working with either of them.

She also wanted to know if Drake was as chauvinistic and obstinate as he seemed to her. Sometimes first impressions weren't accurate. And she had to admit her attitude toward men was a bit skewed right now. She wanted to blame Ethan, her ex-fiancé, but she knew she was the one responsible for her attitude.

Ethan and Addi may have broken her heart, but she was the one allowing that heartbreak to affect her life. She was upset with Ethan for stealing her money to elope with her roommate, the woman Shawn had considered her best friend. She was mad at Addi for her deception as well, but mostly she was irritated with herself for not knowing of their affair. She vowed not to let her guard down or trust anyone enough to permit them to hurt her again.

She knew she should keep an open mind regarding Drake until she got to know him better. She even admitted it was possible he was having a bad day and never meant to come across the way he had. Time would tell.

* * *

After following Drake down a corridor barely wide enough for his shoulders, Shawn was surprised when he pushed aside a curtain hanging in a doorway. A tiny room, made even smaller by Drake's presence, contained two stacks of bunks. There was a porthole above the top bunk on the right and one on the wall opposite the doorway.

"This is the bunkroom." Drake pointed to the bottom berth on the left. "That's JP's. Take your pick of the others."

"I assume he's another hand?" Shawn asked as she looked around.

Drake nodded and turned to leave the bunkroom.

Shawn raised her eyebrows. "Hey, Drake."

When he faced her, she asked, "Which bunk is yours?"

"It doesn't matter. It's only a place to sleep."

Shawn recoiled from his irritated expression. "Take it easy. I was trying to be polite. I figured it would be pretty rude of me to take your bunk and you didn't point out which one was yours."

"I'll sleep on the deck before I'll share a room with you."

His open hostility surprised Shawn. She knew he wasn't pleased but didn't think he'd be so blunt about it.

Before she could respond, he continued in his angry tone. "I don't like you and I don't want you on *The KayLeigh*. I don't know what Dad was thinking, but hiring you was a mistake."

Shawn opened her mouth to retaliate and Drake straightened in the doorway. Shawn could barely see the gray of his eyes as he continued. "I'm not finished. We're not going to be friends. I'll tolerate your presence. But only because Dad has some crazy reason he thinks this is a good idea.

"I know for a fact it's not, and I doubt it'll take him long to realize it either." Drake stepped back and disappeared down the hall, leaving Shawn speechless.

Shawn looked around the room. A couple feet separated the two stacks of bunks, and there were two wall sconces between the beds, one at each level so a switch could be reached from any of the bunks.

She dropped her knapsack on the bottom bunk on the right, already regretting the choices which had brought her here. Would it really have been so bad to stay in Seattle? At least there, she'd been respected.

Snorting, she corrected herself. *Your fiancé eloping with your supposed best friend isn't exactly 'being highly respected'. Turns out life pretty much sucks no matter where you go when you're Shawn Marie Nilsen.*

She was surprised by Drake's lack of manners. The least he could have done was share some information on the other crewmembers. It seemed like a common courtesy, but she was beginning to realize there wouldn't be any politeness toward her from Drake. At least not until he knew she was serious about doing her job.

Even if it killed her, she wouldn't give him the satisfaction of watching her fail. And, she pointed out to herself, she still didn't know whether Drake treated all greenhorns the same way. Obviously, the comments regarding her gender were based on that, but maybe he made all the new hands suffer to test their mettle, like the drill sergeants had done in boot camp.

She wouldn't know until she met the crew, and

chances were slim that she'd meet anyone while she was hiding in the bunkroom. At some point, she'd have to meet them and learn whether they were as bad as Drake. *As bad as Drake seemed*, she corrected herself.

"Might as well get it over with." She pulled on a pair of gloves as she walked back outside.

* * *

Drake and another man were talking at the edge of the deck. She knew they weren't paying any attention to her, so she stopped and looked them over. Drake was a couple inches taller than her and thin.

Surprised to find herself thinking he was good-looking, she started to smile before neutralizing her expression. The last thing she needed was to be attracted to her boss's son, and he'd made it perfectly clear they weren't going to be friends. She wondered whether they'd even reach the point of civility toward one another.

With a shake of her head, Shawn turned her attention to the other man. She guessed he was probably close to six-four and solid all the way through. He wore faded jeans and an old, stained sweatshirt, frayed at the cuffs, and beat-up leather boots. His dark hair curled around his collar and the honey-colored skin of his face.

When the two of them noticed Shawn, Drake turned his face away and the other man smiled. Shawn swallowed hard and approached them, hoping with all of her being this guy might be decent, but expecting him to share Drake's attitude. When Drake sneered instead of introducing them, she turned toward the larger man and said, "I'm Shawn."

"Hey, I'm JP." His voice was friendly. "Drake didn't mention he was dating anyone."

Shawn shook her head in confusion. "What's that supposed to mean?"

"Not a chance in hell," Drake said at the same time. "Dad hired her. Obviously, he's lost his mind."

Shawn tried not to squirm under JP's perusal. His

eyes seemed to bore right through her and she wondered if he could tell she was hiding something—or did he also think she was incapable of doing the job?

"Where you from?" JP asked.

"Seattle, most recently," Shawn replied.

"Why you here?"

Shawn swallowed and peeked at Drake from the corner of her eye. He was resting against a stack of crab pots, thumbs hooked in the front pockets of his jeans. Beneath the smug look on his face, he seemed interested in Shawn's response.

She wasn't going to tell them how Ethan and Addi eloped or that she wanted to run away from her life. All she wanted was to do her job. Uncertain what to say, Shawn resorted to her standby for awkward times—sarcasm verging on the edge of meanness. "I wondered what it'd be like to surround myself with jerks. For some reason it seemed like a good idea at the time."

Without waiting for a response, she turned on her heel and stalked to the bow of the boat. She wrapped her hands around the railing and gazed across the harbor. When her hands started to ache, she forced herself to let go and looked around with interest.

The stack of the crab pots covered most of the deck with narrow walkways connecting the bow and stern of the boat. Weaving through the maze, she stepped around the wheelhouse, saw JP bent over the rail and retreated, not ready for another confrontation yet.

"Hey."

Shawn turned, knowing she hadn't made things easy with her sarcastic response to his question earlier but she hoped for the best.

"Come here," JP said.

Shawn lifted her chin and approached him, preparing for more verbal sparring. At least she hoped it would only be verbal. She relaxed when she looked over the railing and saw a sea lion next to the boat. JP must not be too terrible if he liked animals.

JP dropped a chunk of fish into the sea lion's open

mouth. When it barked in approval, JP spoke to it. "Hush. You know I'm not supposed to feed you."

The sea lion huffed quietly.

"Good boy." JP glanced at Shawn. "He hangs around and I give him a snack before each trip." He held out a bucket of fish.

Shawn selected a piece and dropped it to the sea lion as she asked, "How do you know it's the same one?"

"A scar on his back." JP held a fish up so the sea lion had to jump to get it. "See?" he asked when it splashed back into the water.

Shawn watched him dole out the remainder of the fish, unsure what to say, yet curious why he'd called her over.

"What's your last name?" JP asked without looking at her.

"Nilsen," she said with dread. Would he recognize her surname? And if he did, what would his reaction be? She was glad she hadn't bothered unpacking yet. If this guy said something to the captain revealing her identity, she might find herself unemployed.

"Your grandpa from around here?"

Apparently, JP did recognize the name and Shawn jerked her head toward him to see his reaction. His mouth had curved into a wide smile, which Shawn was familiar with. She wondered why she hadn't known him earlier. His features were the same, but he wasn't gangly for his height anymore. He'd filled out quite a bit and his hair was shorter and darker. A decade will change anyone, but she was surprised at her lack of recognition and even more amazed he'd known her.

Shawn thought she'd changed a lot since she'd last seen him, giving up her teen-angst look of black hair and baggy clothes. Her hair was now its natural brown color and she dressed for comfort. "JP," she said slowly.

"Jarvis Parker," they said together.

"Wow. Of all the boats I could be on, I end up on one with somebody I know." Shawn tensed again, wondering if JP would tell Cap and Drake who her grandfather was. She wasn't ashamed of it; she just didn't want any special treatment when they learned she owned a fishing boat. Knowing she was going to be sharing a tiny bunkroom with someone she'd had a crush on ten years ago added more tension.

"How strange is that?"

"It's definitely weird." If Shawn believed in it, she'd question fate.

"If you want to fish, why aren't you on your grandpa's boat?"

Shawn bit her lower lip. "He died a few months ago."

"I know. I was sorry to hear."

Shawn remained silent. If he knew her grandpa was dead, why would he expect her to be on *Poseidon*? Did he really think she'd go out on the boat without her grandpa?

"You keeping his boat?" JP turned his gaze to her from the sea lion.

Shawn wasn't ready to make JP a confidant, but she'd never been good at lying or keeping secrets. "I haven't decided yet."

"What do your folks want to do with it?"

"They don't get a vote. He left everything to me."

"Guess you're set."

"Yeah, I guess," Shawn said even though she didn't feel set. She had no idea what she wanted out of life. She didn't know where she wanted to be. She didn't feel like she knew anything about anything right now. "How'd you know it was me?" she asked after a moment of silence.

"How many other female Shawns do you suppose there are in the world?"

JP laughed at her shrug. "And how many of those do you suppose are Nilsens?"

Shawn turned and rested her hip against the railing. "I'm surprised you'd even remember my name."

"Why wouldn't I?"

Shawn paused. How could she say she doubted she'd mattered enough for him to remember her without sounding like the fifteen-year-old girl she'd been when she last saw him? She forced a smile. "I'm surprised, that's all."

She was more uncomfortable with every passing minute.

JP grabbed her left wrist and pushed up the sleeve of her jacket. "Besides, I'd have known the minute I saw that." He tapped the long, jagged scar on her forearm.

Shawn drew her arm away and tugged her jacket back down when she spotted Drake approaching.

"Does he know who you are?" JP asked under his breath.

Shawn shook her head and remembered her worry about JP revealing her identity. She would never ask anyone to lie for her. If he felt it was necessary to tell Cap or Drake who she was, she'd face the consequences. She hadn't lied in reference to her family; she simply hadn't offered any information beyond what was asked.

JP raised his voice so Drake would hear him. "According to Simba, we'll have a good catch."

"The only thing that sea lion told you was he's too lazy to find his own food." Drake stopped in front of Shawn. "JP's married."

"So?" Shawn asked.

"So, don't think you can get him to do your work by flirting with him."

Shawn batted her eyelashes at JP. "I was sure he was man enough to do both our jobs."

JP chuckled and Shawn turned back to Drake. "It's going to be a long trip if you do nothing but glare at me."

"So?" he mimicked her previous response. "I'm sick of you already. And I'm certain it's going to be a long trip."

No longer surprised by his obvious dislike for her but curious what irked him so much; she pushed away from the rail. "No point. Nice to meet you, JP." She spoke as she walked away, fighting the urge to look back and see Drake's reaction.

* * *

Shawn approached Cap in the wheelhouse. "I don't think this is going to work out—"

"Too late," Cap interrupted and pointed out the window. Drake and JP were coiling the lines they'd just cast off. "We're on our way." Cap glanced at his watch. "It's almost sixteen hours to where we're headed. This is probably the last chance you'll have to get more than a few hours of sleep at a time, so I suggest you hit the sack and rest up."

Shawn gaped at him. This was it. No way out now. Maybe things would change, but she had a suspicion no one on *The KayLeigh*, except maybe JP, was going to make her feel welcome here. She would do her job and hope for the best. Pitying herself wouldn't make the situation any better. She went down into the galley where she saw JP and Drake entering from the deck.

"Coffee?" JP asked.

"No, thanks." Shawn walked past them and out the door they'd entered. She'd intended to be friendly, but decided she needed to be away from Drake more. At least for now.

* * *

As Drake and JP settled onto the benches surrounding the table in the galley, Cap called down from the wheelhouse, "Drake, I need to talk to you."

"In trouble already?" JP asked his longtime friend.

"God only knows," Drake replied, taking his mug and climbing the steep stairs from the galley to the wheelhouse.

Classical music played from the small speakers in the corners of the ceiling. Without speaking, Drake glanced over Cap's shoulder and checked the computer screens and radar, easily understanding the various monitors. With a nod of satisfaction, he sank into the chair next to Cap's. The brown leather, worn soft over time, had enough give to shape itself to Drake's body as he propped his feet on the edge of the desk, crossing his ankles.

He was comfortable here. He'd spent more time on *The KayLeigh* than he had on land and he loved it. Entering the wheelhouse soothed his nerves most of the time and today was no different. Even as angry as he was with Cap for hiring a woman, some, but not all, of his irritation faded as he settled into the chair.

Cap sipped from a coffee mug and when he set it down, he looked away from his controls out the window. Drake waited in silence, knowing there was nothing he could do to make Cap speak before he was good and ready. When Cap turned from the window, Drake dropped his feet to the floor and swiveled his chair to face his father.

Cap met Drake's gaze and, before Drake had a chance to speak, stated, "I'm the captain. I make the hiring decisions." He took another swallow of his coffee before he continued.

"Mike called me a few days ago to ask if I had any openings. Someone who'd been in the Guard with him was coming up and needed a job. His friend was down on their luck, but he vouched for them, saying they're a hard worker and good on the water even though they'd never fished before."

"How good?" Drake asked.

"One of the calmest, coolest people in an emergency, he said."

"He didn't mention this person—this Coast Guard god—was a woman? And you agreed to hire them sight unseen?"

"I knew she was a woman and I met her before I hired her."

In Drake's experience, Cap had always made decent hiring decisions before. Grudgingly, Drake admitted to himself his father may have in this case too, but something about Shawn made Drake uncomfortable and he couldn't pinpoint what it was.

"What makes her so great?" Drake asked, trying to remain calm. He knew flying off the handle wouldn't make Cap agree with his opinion.

"I have a feeling she'll be good for *The KayLeigh*." Cap looked at the multiple computer screens and adjusted their course automatically. "Besides, we needed a hand."

Drake stood and moved to the window before saying, "It's bad luck to have a woman on a boat, Dad."

Drake stared out the window as Cap replied. "Don't give me that crap, boy. Why do you believe in those old wives' tales? Haven't you ever stepped on a crack? Walked under a ladder?"

Unwilling to dismiss his superstitions, Drake spoke quietly. "What about Bjorn?" He turned from the window to meet his father's gaze, not even trying to hide the pain in his expression.

"A tragedy."

"Kirima," Drake replied, blaming his dead friend's wife.

"An accident that could have happened anywhere. With or without a woman on board." Cap stood. "I need some more coffee," he said and disappeared down the stairs to the galley leaving Drake alone with his thoughts.

Drake had warned Bjorn he had a bad feeling regarding his father-in-law's boat, but Bjorn had laughed at Drake and called him a worrywart. It was the last time they spoke. When Drake learned the boat had gone down with his boyhood friend, he'd been devastated. He still held himself responsible because he hadn't been able to change Bjorn's mind. If Bjorn had heeded Drake's warning, he'd still be alive.

It wasn't the only time Drake had a premonition of something bad happening. It was the most vivid though. He had a similar feeling now and didn't know why, but suspected the new hand, Shawn, would somehow bring disaster to *The KayLeigh*. He knew he'd never be able to change Cap's mind. Cap was optimistic to the extreme, where Drake tended to see the bad in everything.

When Cap returned to the wheelhouse with his steaming mug, he said, "Say your piece."

Drake turned from the window. "I don't trust her," he said tersely.

"Why?"

"She's hiding something." There was something in her attitude and personality that rubbed him the wrong way. It wasn't that she'd punched him, either. The way her eyes flicked around, never meeting his when they spoke, made him wonder what she was hiding.

Crab fishing was strenuous, even when you had a crew that worked well together. Anyone who didn't do their fair share made everyone else's job that much harder.

He was surprised by her strength when she'd punched him but suspected most of the force was due to anger. If she stayed angry, she might be able to do the work, but he still didn't think it was a good idea.

Cap's voice broke into Drake's thoughts. "We've all got secrets. It doesn't mean we're bad people."

"You know what it's like to work with someone you don't trust."

"I do, but we'd have that with any new hand, male or female. There's always a period of getting to know and trust each other."

Drake took a deep breath. "It's dangerous."

Cap slammed his hand down on the arm of his chair. "You think I'd risk my crew? I've done this longer than you've been alive. I know the risks involved." He cleared his throat and continued in a calmer voice. "I don't think it's going to be as bad as you say. She's been on boats before. She knows what can happen. Remember, she was in the Coast Guard with Mike. And I respect his opinion."

"I don't trust her."

"Well, you're going to have to learn to."

Drake spun around. "This is wrong. Something bad is going to happen. I can feel it."

Cap dismissed Drake's statement with a wave of his hand. "You know it's just opening day jitters. You want something, someone, to poke at and blame. It wouldn't matter who I hired, you'd still be griping about it."

"Griping? Wait until we get out there. She's not going to be any help. You'll be complaining because of how slow we're pulling pots."

Cap chortled. "I'll be bitching about how slow you're working no matter what. It's what the captain does."

After a few seconds of silence, Cap pushed on. "That

it? You're not going to change my mind, but I'll listen to what you have to say."

"I don't think she can pull her weight."

"Why? Because she's a woman?"

"Plus she's small. You wouldn't hire a kid. She's practically the same size I was when I was twelve."

"And when you were twelve, you were always begging to crab with me."

"And you always said I was too small," Drake said, thinking Cap had made his point for him.

"I said you were too young. There's a difference. And," he held up a hand to prevent Drake from responding. "You're my son. I wasn't willing to take any risks with your safety."

"That still doesn't explain why you hired her."

"I was friends with her grandfather. I didn't want her to end up on a boat with a bunch of asses who'd take advantage of her." Cap glowered. "She isn't aware that I know who she is and you're not going to say anything about it, either."

"Who's her grandfather?"

"It doesn't matter. I told him I'd look after her if she ever came up here. If she wants you to know who her grandpa was, she'll tell you herself."

Drake had said all he could. He'd used the few valid arguments he had and he wasn't going to reiterate his bad feelings regarding her and *The KayLeigh*. He knew Cap would continue to believe it was opening day jitters even though Drake was never nervous about fishing.

"Then I don't want to hear anything more about it. You've had your chance to voice your opinion, and once you leave here the topic's closed."

"Your wife called this morning." Drake's voice was barely above a whisper.

"Is that what has you frothing at the mouth?" Cap asked.

Drake sneered. "It sure didn't put me in the right frame of mind for working with a woman."

When Cap didn't respond, Drake continued. "She's

coming up."

"When?" Cap asked and concentrated on steering the boat between two buoys in the harbor.

Drake knew he was pretending because Cap could exit the harbor at Kodiak with his eyes closed. It definitely didn't take the amount of focus Cap was using.

"A couple of days." Drake watched his father for an indication of his feelings.

Expressionless, Cap spoke. "Good. It's time you two worked out your differences."

"Work out our differences?" Drake's voice rose. "As far as I'm concerned, she can rot in hell."

Cap shook his finger at Drake. "Don't talk that way about your mother, boy."

"Mother? She's not a mother. Mothers don't leave their kids or split up their families."

Cap's voice was quiet, but his anger was clear from his flashing eyes and clenched jaw. "She's your mother and you will treat her with respect."

"Like the respect she's treated our family with?"

"You don't know the whole story," Cap said, all the anger gone from his voice.

"I know she left us. And I don't know why the hell you keep making excuses for her. She hasn't come back in twenty-five years. She doesn't deserve respect from either of us."

When Drake noticed Cap was looking at him with a contemplative expression, he said, "What?"

Cap wiped his hand across his face. "When we get back, you might want to look for a different place to live."

"Why? Are you kicking me out of the house?"

"No, I figured you wouldn't want to live with your parents."

"I don't. You live on the boat."

Cap looked down at the mug in his hand. "Not for much longer. Your mother is coming back permanently."

"What?"

"We're going to make it work."

"Why didn't you do it twenty-five years ago if you

were going to do it? We're fine without her."

"No, we're not fine without her. I still love her and I've been miserable without her. Why do you think we never got divorced?"

"I don't know. Maybe you didn't think she was worth the bother. Maybe you didn't know where she was."

Cap took another sip of coffee. "I knew where she was the whole time."

Drake muttered under his breath.

"Grow up." Cap moved to stand in front of Drake. "I'm pretty sure your life is still full of twists and turns and it's not going to end up the way you planned. If you think you can make things turn out the way you want by sheer stubbornness alone, you're going to be pretty damn miserable."

With a frustrated shake of his head, Drake left the wheelhouse, slamming the door.

* * *

In the bunkroom, Shawn stowed her bag under her bunk and hung her jacket on a wall hook. She collapsed on the bunk and kicked her boots to the floor, comforted by the rocking of the boat.

She'd spent some time on boats. When she was fifteen, she'd grown tired of her father's refusal to answer her questions about his family. After finding her grandfather's address on an old envelope, she ran away from home and spent three months on *Poseidon*, Grandpa's fishing boat. That's how she met JP. He was working for her grandfather when she came to Alaska the first time.

Reliving the past wasn't what Shawn wanted. She wanted to be alone to make her decisions. Her parents believed she had already decided on her grandfather's estate, though she'd never responded when they asked about it. Her father had left Alaska when he was eighteen and never returned. Her mother never met Shawn's grandparents. Grandpa hadn't even known Shawn existed until she showed up on the dock next to *Poseidon*.

He had accepted her instantly and she loved him from the moment she met him. His temper didn't faze her. She enjoyed learning everything he had taught her concerning fishing and Alaska. But as much as she loved her grandfather and *Poseidon*, Shawn knew she couldn't stay with him.

She fought to spend the summer and suspected she'd been allowed to stay only because her parents hoped performing manual labor for three months would make her more appreciative of all they'd given her in life. Their plan had backfired, though. She returned to Minnesota with a cast on her arm the day before her sophomore year, and, ever since, she'd felt the most alive when her muscles ached and her hands were callused.

Tired of the trip down memory lane, Shawn rose from the bunk, wandered into the galley and spotted JP at the counter chopping vegetables. "What are you doing?" she asked as she approached.

"Making supper." JP scooped the vegetables into a bowl of lettuce and tossed it before grabbing a pack of cheese from the fridge. He closed the door and pushed on the bottom of the door with his foot. "It doesn't seal. Make sure you kick the bottom."

"You're the cook?"

"The deckhands take turns. I hope you cook better than Drake."

Shawn enjoyed cooking and her friends were always happy to be invited over for a meal. She didn't feel any need to brag so she said, "I do okay." She watched him. "What are you making?"

"Lasagna, garlic toast, and salad. Nothing special."

"Sounds great to me." Shawn watched as he covered a tray of French bread with mozzarella cheese. When he slid the pan into the oven, she said, "How are they to work for?"

"They're slave drivers. But they're fair. They've never expected more of me than they expect of themselves. Of course, I've known them most of my life, so maybe I'm a bit biased."

"It's a decent boat?"

"Way better than decent." He poured a cup of coffee and offered it to her.

"No, thanks. I don't drink coffee."

"What's your poison?" JP asked.

"What do you think?"

"Still on that chocolate milk kick?"

Shawn laughed, not surprised he remembered. He had teased her incessantly about her love for chocolate milk during the time they'd spent together on *Poseidon*.

"You're in luck." JP poured a mug of milk, then set a canister of chocolate powder on the counter in front of her.

Shawn mixed a cup and settled into the corner of the orange vinyl bench that formed a U-shape around the table. "So what's new with you? Been fishing all this time?"

JP slid into the booth across from her. "Not steadily. I spent some time trying to be a normal land-dwelling person. It didn't work out and Cap was looking for a hand, so I hired on. Been here the last four years."

"What did you try to do?"

"I got a degree in aquatic biology."

"And you're still on a fishing boat?"

"Yeah, it's more fun than studying what's in the water. What have you been up to?"

Shawn toyed with her mug, contemplating how much to tell him. Even though she knew him ten years ago, she didn't necessarily trust him. Besides she didn't need anyone's sympathy. She just wanted to do her job and earn some money. "Not much," she said, and glanced up at JP.

JP frowned. "Got it. None of my business. That's cool." He moved to stand.

"JP, wait," Shawn said and reached out to touch his arm.

He stopped next to the table and met her gaze.

She shifted her eyes away and spoke. "It's not you. It's..." Her voice faded and after a moment of silence, she continued. "My life is pretty much a mess right now and I don't want to talk about it."

"I get it." He opened the oven door to peek in. "Five minutes to go."

Shawn propped her chin in her hand as she watched him, hoping she hadn't messed up any chance of rekindling their friendship by being so close-mouthed.

"What'd your parents say about your arm?" JP asked as he turned back toward her.

"Obviously a fishing boat was no place for a fifteen-year-old girl." Shawn paused and laughed at the memory. "And maybe I'd learned my lesson."

"What kind of lesson?" JP set the salad bowl on the table in front of her.

"I guess I was supposed to acknowledge they were smarter than me."

"Did you?"

"No." Shawn stood and opened cupboard doors until she discovered plates. She took a stack and when she turned, Drake stood right inside the galley, jaw set.

Shawn deposited the dishes on the table. Already weary of the tension every time she was around Drake, she forced a smile and said, "JP made lasagna."

"Good for JP," Drake replied and settled into the corner of the bench.

JP dished up four servings of lasagna, sat next to Drake and dug into his food.

Shawn slid into the booth opposite Drake and stared at her plate. Drake didn't look like Ethan, but he still reminded her of him. Some of his mannerisms were the same, like how he ran his hand over his hair. And how he clenched his jaw in anger, like he was literally biting back his words. Realizing she was making Drake pay for Ethan's mistakes because they had a few similar behaviors, Shawn vowed to give him a chance as a person.

After what seemed like an eternity of silence, Shawn commented on the sweatshirt Drake wore. "Calgary seems to have a good team this year. Do you think they have a chance at the cup?" Being raised in Minnesota, hockey was the one sport Shawn followed closely. She thought Drake might loosen up if she could find a topic of discussion they both had an interest in.

Drake held her gaze for a few seconds before returning his attention to his food. Shawn swallowed, questioning her resolve already. It wasn't going to be easy to change his opinion of her, but she reminded herself how much she liked a challenge.

Cap came into the galley, filled his cup from the coffee pot and sat next to Shawn. "Looks good," he said to JP, and ate his helping of pasta without another word. As he scooped more lasagna onto his plate, he looked at Drake. "What do you think of heading up past St. Paul Island?"

"You're the boss." Shawn could hear the irritation in Drake's voice and she barely knew him.

JP glanced from Drake to Cap and back, then at Shawn who quickly broke eye contact.

The rest of the meal was strained. JP attempted to make them laugh a couple times, but the only reaction was a sympathetic smile from Shawn as she wondered again how they all got along before she joined the crew.

Cap finished his meal first and, after thanking JP for cooking, returned to the wheelhouse.

Shawn slid out of the booth and started cleaning the galley. She'd filled the sink with water when Drake appeared next to her.

"I'll do it," he said.

"It's not a problem. I can do the dishes," Shawn said, and started adding dishes to the soapy water.

"I said I'd do it." Drake shouldered her away from the sink.

"We take turns washing up. Drake likes to clean up when I cook because I'm messy and then he doesn't have to be outside working." JP mumbled around a mouthful of food.

Drake raised an eyebrow and laughed at JP. "Except you're so slow I finish before you're even done eating."

"I can help," Shawn offered again, wishing she could join in the teasing banter between the two of them.

Drake glared at her.

"Or not," Shawn said and turned away. "Thanks for supper, JP. It was great.

"You'd think he'd be mature enough to be civil," she grumbled under her breath as she returned to the bunkroom. Temper flares she could handle, but Shawn didn't know how to deal with silent hatred. She assumed the problem was as he'd stated; she was a woman. And there was no way she could change that.

She removed her sweatshirt and dropped it on the floor before stretching out on the bunk and closing her eyes. Maybe a nap would make her more resilient to Drake's treatment. And if it didn't, at least she didn't have to think while she was asleep.

* * *

Drake walked to the bunkroom, angry he had to wake Shawn. He knew he was holding her gender against her. He wouldn't have a problem if JP were catching a nap, or any of the other hands he'd worked with over the years. He even acknowledged it made sense to sleep whenever you could on a fishing vessel because there were many nights when more than two or three hours would be unlikely. He and JP didn't nap on the trip out because they were too excited to be on the water.

The entire problem with Shawn was her gender. Right now, the only thing she had going in her favor was punching him. He was certain from the look in her eyes the act had terrified her and she hadn't backed down. He'd never admit it, but she'd impressed him.

He pushed aside the curtain that hung in the bunkroom doorway and saw she'd taken the bottom berth on the right, across from JP's. The bed Drake normally used. Irritation rose, but he tamped it down. It was his fault, and his alone. She had asked which was his, and he'd said it didn't matter.

He leaned his shoulder against the doorjamb and looked her over. She was lying on her stomach, feet toward the door. He noted she was smart enough to wear wool socks, and high-quality boots sat next to the bunk. Moving his gaze over her legs, which seemed long for such a tiny woman, he paused to look at her butt for a few seconds, where the denim had all but disintegrated near the corners of the pockets.

He shifted his gaze up her body, past the strip of pale skin showing between her low-riding jeans and tank top. Her right arm curled under her head; the left hung off the bunk. Drake was surprised to see a jagged scar nearly four inches long on her forearm and wondered what had caused it.

She reminded him of Kirima, Bjorn's widow. They were close to the same size and height, but the physical similarities ended there. Kirima was Inuit and her features showed it. Shawn's features were delicate in comparison and her complexion was pale. Her smooth skin was going to take a hell of a beating from the weather, and she would be in a lot of pain from the drying and cracking in a matter of days if she wasn't prepared. He considered mentioning it, but his bad mood over-ruled his normally helpful nature.

Knowing Kirima his entire life, Drake recognized the same attitude in Shawn. The only difference he noticed so far was Shawn didn't captain one of the largest fishing boats docked in Kodiak. Kirima hadn't backed down from a fight in her life and Bjorn always claimed he loved her attitude most about her. Drake never understood the attraction.

The women Drake dated were easy-going. None of them ever stood up to him, even to disagree about where they wanted to go for dinner. That was fine with Drake. He spent the majority of his time fishing with stubborn men. When he wasn't working, he didn't want to deal with attitude.

Angry that he was intrigued by her, Drake kicked the wall next to her bunk and snarled, "Get out of bed. It's time to drop pots."

Shawn rolled over and met his gaze. "You get your fill?"

Drake jerked his head back a fraction of an inch, like he'd been hit again. "What are you talking about?"

"You've been standing there for a while."

Drake raised his hand to the back of his head and scratched. *How could she possibly know how long I've been here?* With a frown, he said, "Like hell."

"Yeah. You have." Shawn sat up and raked her hair away from her face. She fished a clip from her pocket and fastened her hair back. "I heard you."

Drake guffawed. "In your dreams."

Shawn stood and pulled the sweatshirt from the floor over her head. Drake cursed himself for noticing her flat stomach when her tank top rode up. She pulled on rain gear and jammed both feet into her boots.

"Besides, I could smell you."

Drake realized his hand was still on the back of his head, and he lowered it in what he hoped was a casual manner. "Now I know you're full of shit."

"Old Spice makes me want to puke." She pulled her gloves and hat on and pushed past him in the doorway.

"Sure it's Old Spice?" Drake taunted.

"Yeah. I recognize it. Kind of hard not to when you apparently bathe in it."

Drake gawked at her as she walked away. When he noticed he was still standing in the door trying to decide whether she was right about the amount of Old Spice he used, he cursed and kicked the wall again, wondering why her opinion mattered to him at all.

* * *

Unsure of herself but trying not to let it show, Shawn approached JP, who was hunched next to a tub of frozen fish. "What do I do?" she asked.

JP looked up. "Grind fish and fill bait jars." He nodded at the plastic tub of fish. "We're using cod for bait." Grabbing a large plastic jar with holes drilled in it; he held it under a metal chute and flipped a switch with his other hand.

Shawn gagged at the smell as the jar filled with chopped fish. JP laughed at her expression and turned the bait grinder off. "You'll get used to it soon enough."

Shawn swallowed and fought to control her urge to vomit as JP explained that the jars were filled roughly halfway and the scent attracted the crabs. "The crabs won't actually get any of the fish you're grinding. We hang a whole cod in the trap so the crabs have something to feed on, otherwise they'll end up fighting and injuring one another."

"Makes sense," Shawn said and struggled to find a way to hold the jar, flip the switch and keep the fish bits flowing into the jar instead of up into her face.

"You'll figure it out. It takes a little practice," JP said as he moved away.

Shawn didn't intend to fail the first chore given to her, and, if she kept her back to Drake, she didn't have to acknowledge his presence. Once she'd filled the pile of bait jars, she turned to watch as Drake and JP wrestled a pot onto a low bench near the rail.

Drake opened the door of the trap and pulled the buoys and line out, while JP grabbed a bait jar from the pile beside Shawn, clipped it inside, picked a whole cod from another tub, sliced it down the middle with a quick motion, ran a hook through its head and hung it next to the bait jar. Drake closed and latched the trap, and then backing to the side, he pushed a button on a control panel causing hydraulics to lift the bench and the pot to slide over the side of the boat as JP tossed the buoys and lines after it.

Shawn watched them hook the next pot and lift it with a crane, before sliding it into place and opening the door. This time when JP reached for the bait jar, she handed it to him. On the third one, she hung the bait jar in place. She had to slide into the pot on her back and hang the jar and cod over her head because of her short reach. When some of the innards fell from a split cod into her mouth, she rolled to the side and retched as Drake laughed. She shot a nasty look at him but kept working, making sure her mouth remained closed. By the tenth time she repeated the process, Shawn no longer had to think of how to fasten the bait jars in the traps. By the fifteenth pot, the men weren't slowing their process for her; she was keeping up.

After they dropped twenty pots, Cap called over the intercom, "Come on in. We'll let 'em soak and check back in a few hours."

JP draped an arm around Shawn's shoulders and the other around Drake's. "Looks like we've got ourselves quite a team."

Drake waved him off. "Don't bet on it," he said and disappeared toward the wheelhouse.

Shawn ducked from under JP's arm. "What is his problem? Is he always like this, or is he on his best behavior because of me?"

"Something's bothering him."

"Yeah. Me."

Chapter Two

Shawn went into the galley, surprised when she looked at the clock. They'd dropped pots for six hours. She hung her jacket on a peg and kicked off her boots, heading to the sink to wash her hands and face. Only then did she acknowledge her empty stomach.

When Drake entered the room, she was beating eggs in a bowl. "What do you want in your omelet?" she asked.

"Doesn't matter."

"Just answer the question." Shawn demanded, holding a cast iron pan in her hand.

"I'm too tired to care. Sawdust would be fine." Drake reached for a cup, filled it with water from the teapot, dropped in a bag, and flopped down at the table.

"Here." Shawn slammed an omelet-heaped plate in front of him. "Toast will be done in a minute." She turned back to the stove and quickly made three more ham and cheese omelets, handing them out as JP and Cap entered the galley.

No one spoke until they were finished eating and Drake said, "Thanks."

Shawn carried her plate to the sink where JP was washing up. "Want some help?" she offered.

"Nah. You done good." JP nudged her away from the sink. "Get some sleep."

With a yawn, Shawn turned, stripping off her sweatshirt on her way out of the galley and her jeans the instant she was in the bunkroom. Wearing her long johns, wool socks and a tank top, she fell onto her bunk and was asleep in seconds, barely managing to drag her unzipped sleeping bag over her body.

* * *

Shawn jerked awake when she heard her name spoken. She rolled to the side and saw JP buttoning his jeans. "Come on," he said. "We've got about twenty minutes before we start pulling pots."

Shawn stretched, got out of bed, pulled on the clothes from yesterday and braided her hair to keep it out of her face. When she entered the galley, Drake handed her a plate of French toast.

"Morning," she said, opening the fridge.

"Coffee's hot," Drake said.

Surprised Drake had been almost cordial, Shawn sat next to JP at the table, downed her breakfast and started tidying the cooking area. She chuckled when she realized Drake cleaned up after himself as he cooked. All that remained for her was washing the eating utensils and one pan. Maybe he wasn't such a jerk after all. Cap and JP left the galley, and Shawn wiped down the stove and counter.

As soon as Drake finished his breakfast, she washed his dishes. "Thanks for breakfast. It was good."

Drake grunted as he filled an insulated mug with hot water and dropped in a couple tea bags. "More mugs in the cupboard," he said.

"I don't drink tea."

"There's plenty of coffee."

"That either," Shawn responded as she realized she could easily like him.

"You will soon enough." Drake pulled on his jacket and left the galley carrying his cup of tea.

* * *

Shawn followed, thinking this might not be such a horrible experience. She shoved her arms into her sleeves, slid her hands into her gloves, and approached JP at the bait grinder where he'd finished filling the empty bait jars.

Even though Drake hadn't growled at her yet today, she still preferred JP's tutelage.

"What do I do?" she asked, rocking from foot to foot, unable to stand still.

"You fish." JP punched her lightly in the arm. "Calm down. You're going to be fine." He pointed as Drake threw a hook into the water and reeled it back in, snagging a line. He wove the line through a pulley and pressed a button on the control panel. The motor whirred and JP coiled the line as it came through the machine. When the pot was raised above the deck of the boat, Drake released the button and helped JP force it onto the pot launcher.

After opening the trap, they raised it with the hydraulic crane to dump the crabs onto the sorting table. Once the pot was empty, JP baited it and closed it before Drake hit another button to launch it over the side of the boat. Drake tossed the buoys and line after it, as JP motioned Shawn forward to the table of crabs and explained how to sort them. Shawn struggled to keep up until Cap's voice came over the speaker. "Buoy."

Shawn looked up and the entire process was repeated. This time she was waiting to slide into the trap and hang fresh bait as soon as the crabs were out. She helped fasten the door shut and began sorting as JP and Drake launched the pot.

Shawn didn't realize what time it was. Didn't think about anything other than whether or not each crab was big enough to keep. She even got to the point where the icy metal of the crab pot didn't make her flinch when she slid in. And she no longer bothered to wipe the slime from her face. There was no sense wasting the energy; there would be more fish guts on her in a matter of minutes. She was surprised when JP shoved an energy bar into her hand between pots.

"Lunch," he said and gulped down a bottle of water.

"Thanks." Shawn finished the bottle of water JP passed her as fast as he had drank his and ate the bar in three bites. She was still chewing the last mouthful when she slid into the next pot to bait it.

A while later, as they launched a pot, Cap called over the intercom, "That's all of them."

JP left Shawn and Drake on the deck sorting the crabs, while he hauled the bait back into the freezer until tomorrow.

Shawn smiled at Drake and said, "That was fun."

"Fun? What kind of drugs are you on?" Drake asked before turning away.

Shawn raised her hands in a gesture of defeat. "Guess you're a jerk all of the time. This morning, when you were almost nice, you must not have been feeling well."

"Get over yourself already." Drake fastened the cover on the live well and headed toward the galley.

"What's your problem?" Shawn asked.

Drake spun around, squinting against the spray of water Shawn felt hitting the back of her jacket. "Do we really need to go over this again? Don't you remember?"

"I thought maybe you'd grown up in the past eighteen hours and realized how stupid you're being."

"Stupid? You want to talk stupid?" Drake raised his hand and poked her in the breastbone. "Stupid is coming to Alaska and risking an entire crew's life to have a good time. We're not out here for fun; this is our life."

Shawn matched his gaze. She was tired and irritable and had forgotten her intent of killing Drake with kindness. At this point, she wanted to kill him. When he attempted to jab her again, she knocked his hand to the side and said, "I don't have the slightest idea how, or even if, your mind works. I didn't come up here for fun, not that it's any of your business. I came up here to work, and that's what I'm doing. I'm working my ass off and, as amazing as it is, I actually did enjoy today. Maybe 'fun' isn't the right word, but it certainly wasn't the hell you try to portray it as. Do I threaten your masculinity so much you have to be a complete ass all the time? Is it possible that maybe we could be civil to each other?"

Noticing the grin on his face, she asked, "What?"

He nodded at her hand. "You going to use that?"

She looked down at her clenched fist, then at him,

fully intending to continue verbally assaulting him. "I'd like to..." Her voice faded when she saw he was smiling.

She narrowed her eyes and tried to figure out what he was up to. She assumed he was messing with her. But man, was his smile gorgeous. His entire face was open and welcoming, gray eyes sparkling with amusement. Shocked by her thoughts, Shawn backed away—from him and the concept—shaking her head.

As his smile faded, Drake spoke in a smooth, quiet voice. "I don't want you here. You might have done okay today, but wait. You're going to get so tired you can barely move and the pots will still need to be pulled." His gaze was intent. "You're going to fail."

Chapter Three

Shawn hung her gear near the galley before moving to the sink to wash up. She guzzled a mug of water, then looked at JP.

He whistled while he cooked supper. "Potatoes, sausage, eggs, biscuits and gravy," he answered before she could ask what he was making.

"Good God, how can you have so much energy?" she moaned, slumping against the cupboard.

"Coffee." He took a swallow from his mug. "It's got more caffeine than chocolate milk." He stirred the potatoes frying in the pan. "I saw you and Drake talking. Did he actually smile?"

"I don't know. And right now I don't care. I thought he was going to be decent, but then, suddenly, he's back in jerk mode."

"He's pretty serious about fishing. It's all he's ever wanted to do."

"So? It's not like I'm going to get in the way of that." Shawn straightened and set the table, then refilled her water mug.

"He's trying to save enough money to buy his own boat." JP carried the pan to the table and portioned the potatoes equally on the plates.

Shawn yawned. "I still don't see how I'm affecting his future in any way."

"You could." JP dumped the rest of the food into bowls and motioned Shawn to the booth. She sat and he settled in across from her. He lowered his voice. "You could sell him *Poseidon* if you decide not to keep it."

Shawn jerked her attention from her plate to JP's face. "Why would I do that?"

"You'd make your life a lot easier if you told him who you are."

"Why? So he can be nice to me to get a good deal? I don't think so." Shawn looked over her shoulder when she heard footsteps and saw Cap enter the galley.

Cap went to the sink to wash his hands and Shawn threatened JP with her gaze.

As Cap sat next to him, Shawn hoped JP would keep her secret.

Cap smiled at Shawn. "You did good, girl."

Shawn bristled at being called 'girl', but calmed when Cap nudged JP with his elbow. "Didn't she, boy?"

JP swallowed and said, "She did. Almost like she knew what she was doing."

Shawn's gaze flicked toward JP, worried he was going to say something she didn't want him to say.

"Nah. I'd guess she's a quick learner and a hard worker. That's what I like to see when I hire a new hand," Cap said.

When Drake entered the galley, Shawn rushed to finish her meal before he sat down, so she wouldn't have to remain beside him while he ate. Her plate was still half full when he slid into the booth next to her.

Shawn shut her eyes for a few seconds and tried to ignore how close she was to someone who disliked her so intensely, before returning her attention to her food.

"What do you think, son? Do I know how to pick 'em or what?" Cap asked as he mopped up the last of his gravy with a biscuit.

Drake looked up from his plate and met Cap's eyes. "That depends on what you're talking about."

"Hands," Cap replied.

Shawn fidgeted in her seat, not liking where the conversation was going. She also didn't want to be so close to Drake. He smelled like a man who'd worked outside all day. A hint of Old Spice lingered when he reached in front of her for the pepper shaker and grunted in response to Cap's question.

His right arm bumped against her left elbow and she jerked away. "Sorry," she said and switched her fork to her right hand.

"You left-handed?" Cap asked.

"Mostly," Shawn replied. "But I can use either."

"What happened to your arm?"

"Huh?" Shawn looked down expecting to see a bruise or a scrape, but didn't notice anything out of the ordinary.

"How'd you get that scar?" Cap pointed with his coffee mug.

"Oh." Shawn glanced at JP. "I was messing around with a friend and slipped and fell. Compound fracture, took a while to get to the hospital to have it set."

"Must have hurt," JP said.

"A little." Shawn rubbed at the scar and pushed away her plate of unfinished food. "I'm stuffed. If anyone wants what's left..."

JP took a biscuit from her plate and Cap scraped the potatoes onto his. Drake finished his food and, without a word, began cleaning up.

Shawn carried the empty plates to the sink, grabbed a towel, and dried the dishes as Drake set them in the rack.

"I'll do it," he said.

"Yeah, I know." Shawn yawned. "You don't want my help. You've made that clear."

"Go to bed," JP said, and took the towel away from her. "You're making breakfast."

"I can still help clean up."

"We got it," JP said, pushing her toward the hallway.

Shawn left, tired of having her good intentions rebuked. In the bunkroom, she untangled the knots in her hair with her fingers before dragging a brush through it. Exhausted, she wondered if JP would say anything about the story she'd told at supper.

He was the friend she'd been messing around with on *Poseidon*. She developed a serious crush on him, and while trying to get his attention one day, she climbed on the railing around the wheelhouse roof. When she jumped toward the water, she didn't jump far enough, hitting the deck rail and breaking both bones in her forearm, eighteen hours from land and a hospital.

JP was the one who held her while her grandfather tried to maneuver the bones back into place.

When she woke in the hospital, JP was there, holding her hand. She'd asked why and he said she wouldn't let go of his hand, even while unconscious. She'd fought to stay on the boat until JP said he'd go with her on the Coast Guard helicopter.

Shawn had been groggy and her arm hurt. But when JP said how impressed he was that she hadn't cried, she'd been happy. He'd finally noticed her! She'd struggled to lean toward him and JP caught her before she tumbled out of the bed as she wrapped her good arm around his neck. "I love you," she said and kissed him.

That's when her grandfather walked in. And exploded. She tried to explain nothing had happened but Grandpa was too stubborn to listen and fired JP on the spot. The next day he sent Shawn back to her parents and said she couldn't return the following summer because he didn't trust her anymore.

Now she was embarrassed by her childhood actions. She had been mortified to learn JP, the first guy she'd loved, was on *The KayLeigh*. Sharing a bunkroom with him was a little awkward, but thankfully, JP didn't seem to have any qualms and, as of yet, they hadn't had any embarrassing moments of undress.

With disgust at the scent of herself, Shawn changed into her sleepwear before sliding into her bunk, and closed her eyes; happy JP was still willing to be her friend.

* * *

The next morning, Shawn rolled out of bed and pulled on the same jeans she wore the past two days. There wasn't any sense in wearing clean clothes when they'd get filthy anyway. She ran her fingers through her hair and fastened it back, not bothering with a brush.

In the galley, she scanned the contents of the cupboards and decided on pancakes, ham and eggs for breakfast as Drake walked in. He squeezed by her to fill a teakettle and set it on the stove.

Shawn watched him but didn't say anything. If he wanted to talk to her, it was his choice. She turned to the sink and brushed her teeth as the first batch of cakes cooked.

When the kettle whistled, Drake poured a cup of water and dropped in a tea bag. They stood side by side at the stove and she barely had to turn her head from the pancakes she was flipping to look at him. His arm brushed hers and she jerked away, bumping the griddle.

"What?" Drake asked, and turned toward her.

"Nothing," she replied. She wasn't going to tell him how much she'd felt in the fraction of a second their skin had touched. The warmth of his skin wasn't a surprise, but realizing she wanted to feel more of him was. Grabbing plates from the cupboard, she set them on the table and returned to the stove, turning sideways to let Drake pass her. She filled a cup from the ever-present pot of coffee and sipped it. After coughing, she forced herself to swallow.

"Exactly," Drake said. "That's why I drink tea. Their coffee tastes terrible."

Shawn dumped the cup of coffee down the drain and refilled her cup with milk. She flipped pancakes onto a platter and cracked eggs into another pan. "How do you want yours?"

"Doesn't matter."

"Fine," Shawn said. Mornings usually brightened her mood. She was confident she'd be able to win Drake over in time. And even if she couldn't, she wouldn't give up this early in the game. She scrambled the eggs, heated the ham and dumped it all in bowls. Without looking at Drake, she set the food on the table, filled a plate for herself and ate while standing next to the sink.

After she ate and washed her plate, Shawn put on her

gear and went outside. She circled the wheelhouse and headed for the bow of the boat. She sank to the deck and rested against a crab pot, knees to her chest, arms wrapped around her legs and forehead on her knees. Part of her wanted to give up already, but her need to prove her strength and fortitude, if only to herself, precluded her from considering such a possibility.

Since Ethan left eleven days ago, Shawn had second-guessed everything about her life. The last time she could remember being sure about what she was doing was when she was in the Coast Guard. She wasn't about to re-enlist in the Guard but there wasn't any reason for her not to return to Alaska. She suspected if she were on land at this point, she'd curl up in a ball and cry until there was nothing left of her. At least on a crab boat, she'd have work to take her mind off her sadness. And it would help her make an educated decision about *Poseidon*.

After five minutes, she lifted her head from her knees and rolled her shoulders. Her muscles were sore from the physical labor of the past two days, but she enjoyed feeling like she'd done something worthwhile and it was better than brooding about Ethan.

"Time's up. No more moping," Shawn said to herself as she looked around. The fog was lifting to reveal a gray sky. Everything around her was gray, but it was a peaceful gray that reminded her of Drake's eyes. She stood, stretched her arms over her head and forced the thoughts of Ethan and Drake from her mind as she started filling bait jars.

"Hey, what are you doing?" JP asked as he came around the wheelhouse.

"Filling bait jars," she replied without turning toward him.

He fed the frozen cod into the grinder. The two of them worked in silence for a bit before he said, "Something wrong?"

"Nothing important."

"Does it have anything to do with you knowing me?" JP faced her.

"No, that's a little awkward, but it's not what's bothering me." She met his gaze. "Is it a problem for you?"

A flicker of confusion crossed JP's face. "Why do you ask? Am I acting like it's a problem?"

"No." Shawn paused. "JP, I know I was stupid, that is, when you knew me before, but I've changed."

"I wondered when that'd come up."

"When what would come up?"

"The past."

"I want to apologize for getting you in trouble with my grandpa." Shawn searched for the words to make it right. "I never meant... I mean, I didn't..."

"No big deal."

"How can it not be a big deal? You got fired."

"I was leaving for school after that trip, anyway. I just ended up leaving a week earlier than planned. It worked out."

They were both quiet for a while.

"I'm sorry," JP said softly.

Shawn jerked her head around to meet his gaze, and said, "What do you need to apologize for?"

"You were too young and I knew it."

Shawn felt her face grow warm. She didn't want to be reminded how she had thrown herself at him.

"I should have made it clear I wasn't interested." He grinned. "But what guy doesn't like to have a girl chasing after him?"

Shawn suspected the comment was a way to cover up his discomfort in admitting he was flattered. "Don't worry about it."

"Sure?"

"Yeah."

"Okay, I'm going to do the dishes." He glanced at the bait jars. "I'll help you finish these when I'm done."

"Nah, I'll do it. I wouldn't want Drake to think I had too much spare time on my hands."

"He's really not that bad."

Realizing her opinion of Drake made JP

uncomfortable, Shawn forced her mouth into a smile. "Sorry. I'll try to give him a chance."

* * *

During the second shift of pulling pots, JP was retrieving more bait from below deck, leaving Shawn and Drake alone on deck. It was toward the end of the shift and Shawn was exhausted; only her willpower kept her baiting pots and sorting crabs.

Drake threw the hook and reeled in the pot. Shawn cursed and shoved with all her might as Drake lowered it onto the stand, but couldn't get the nine hundred pound pot to move the three inches necessary for it to be secure as they emptied it.

She glanced toward Drake for assistance and knew from the exasperated look on his face as he stepped forward she'd proven his prediction correct; she didn't have the strength needed to do the job. She was making his and JP's life more difficult just because she was a woman and not as strong as they were.

Drake nudged the pot with his shoulder and it moved the quarter of a foot needed as he hit the button on the crane to drop it into the stand.

Angry about her inability to move the full crab pot, Shawn opened the gate and helped shake the crabs onto the sorting table. She turned, grabbed a bait jar and struggled to refasten it. She really didn't want to hear him say "I told you so."

The clip for the bait jar was covered with ice, and Shawn couldn't get it open with her gloves on.

"Hurry up," Drake said, waiting to launch the pot. "We're practically on top of the next one."

Shawn peeled off a glove, baited the trap, slid out of the metal cage and latched the door shut, trying with all her might to make up for the extra work she'd caused Drake. As soon as she stepped back from the launcher, Drake hit the button, sending the pot splashing into the water along with her glove.

Shawn cursed and glanced around the deck for another glove. She didn't see any and the next pot was already over the side. She rushed forward and helped empty the pot with only one glove, after Drake nudged it into place with a smirk in her direction. Every time she fumbled, she could hear Drake's aggravated sigh. Launching the pot went smoothly and Shawn turned to sorting crabs. The water had already iced up on her skin.

She was almost through when one of the crabs latched onto her little finger. Luckily it was a small crab. If it had been the one she'd last tossed in the live well, nearly a foot across the back, she knew her finger would have been pinched right off. As it was, her blood ran off the claw and down the crab's leg.

Reflexively, she shook her hand to dislodge the spiny creature pulled from the depths of the Bering Sea. Instead of letting go, the claw squeezed harder, and Shawn gasped as she fought to keep tears of pain from falling. "Ow," she yelped and looked to Drake for guidance.

"Kill it," he said, continuing to sort crabs. He glanced over his shoulder at the next buoy. "You got about a minute."

Shawn looked around frantically, spotted a hammer and smashed the crab's tiny head. She pried the claws apart, grabbed a rag, and wrapped it around her hand hoping to stem the flow of blood. She was back in time to help Drake pull the next pot and groaned in relief when JP reappeared on deck. She still had to work fast, but it was a more manageable pace. At least the pain was keeping her awake and the rag provided some insulation.

"What happened?" JP asked as they sorted the crabs.

"One of them fought back," Shawn replied, and kept tossing crustaceans into the tank.

"Where's your glove?"

"Lost it." Shawn's answers were short due to her exhaustion and pain.

"Why didn't you get another one?"

"No time to run to the galley to get one."

"All you had to do was ask. We've always got an extra

pair handy."

Shawn looked at JP and tossed her last crab overboard. He seemed upset about something, but she didn't know what. "What's wrong?"

"You could lose a finger. It happens all the time."

Shawn readied the bait while JP and Drake fought the next pot onto the launcher, long red legs poking through the mesh.

JP shook the crabs free of the pot, took the bait jar from Shawn, fastened it in place, latched the door, and turned to Shawn as Drake launched it. "What's your problem?"

"What're you talking about?" Shawn tossed crabs into the holding tank and overboard without looking at JP.

"Why won't you ask for help?"

"I don't need to."

"If you don't clean it out it's going to get infected."

"It's fine." Shawn continued sorting.

"Get inside and clean your finger," JP ordered.

"When we're done with this line."

"Damn it, Shawn. Go. No one's going to yell at you for taking a few minutes to keep your hand from getting infected."

Shawn glanced at Drake who'd been silent since JP's return. She suspected he was listening, even though he wasn't participating in the conversation.

"If you don't, I'll drag you in there and do it myself," JP threatened. "Then he'll bitch about me having to take care of you."

Shawn met Drake's gaze and held it until JP shoved her toward the galley. Shawn went inside while grumbling about being pushed around.

After grabbing the first aid kit, she turned on the faucet, and adjusted the temperature of the water. Without looking at the wound, she lathered her hands with soap and ran the suds over the jagged cuts on opposite sides of her pinkie finger. She glanced out the window and saw they were pulling the next pot. Clenching her jaw, she dried her hand and covered it with gauze, fighting to tape it in place. She yanked on a pair of new gloves and stepped back into the dance on deck.

As they launched the pot, Cap's voice came over the speaker. "Come on in. We're going to drop this load off."

Shawn went inside and removed her gear before getting a drink of water.

"I got supper tonight," JP said when he came into the galley.

"I thought it was Drake's turn."

"If there's time for me to cook, I'll cook. I'll even get breakfast tomorrow. You guys can duke out the cleanup duties."

Shawn left the galley without speaking. She was still upset with JP for forcing her off the deck. She would have been fine to continue. It was only one more pot.

She saw Drake in the hallway. They turned sideways and sidled past one another without saying a word. Shawn went into the bunkroom and removed her sweatshirt. She really wanted to be free from the smell of crab and dead fish and decided she would shower before collapsing in her bunk.

* * *

Drake walked into the head and noticed it was full of steam. He knew JP was cooking and Cap was piloting the boat, which meant Shawn must be in the shower.

The moment he made the connection, he heard her voice. She was talking to herself about him. The scent of lemons wafted out of the shower and Drake inhaled. He knew he should leave; he had no right to stand here and listen. He heard the shower curtain open and Shawn stuck her head out.

Drake backed out of the bathroom, hoping she hadn't seen him, as it would make the trip uncomfortable if she knew he'd been lurking around the bathroom while she showered. He leaned against the wall, wondering why he was spying on her. The thought of her in the steamy shower was tormenting his brain. And other parts of his anatomy, even though he didn't want to admit it.

He acknowledged to himself he would buy her a drink and get to know her better if he'd run into her at a bar. But he hadn't met her at a bar. He'd met her on a crab boat, the last place in the world a woman belonged.

He swallowed and turned, planning to return to the galley, but when he heard the water turn off, he wasn't able to stop himself from glancing over his shoulder. "Oh, man," he said under his breath, realizing the curtain to the bathroom was open enough so he could see her arm reaching from the shower.

Shawn wrapped a towel around her body and rubbed her head with the smaller towel she pulled from her bag. She swiped the mirror with it then dropped it beside her pack and moved to the side so the curtain blocked his view. When he saw the blue towel pool on the floor he turned away, trying not to think of her nakedness and denying the physical reaction he had to the fleeting thought. He moved down the hall and settled into the booth in the galley, knowing he'd see Shawn pass by when she finished in the head.

* * *

"What's up?" JP asked.

"I was going to take a shower but Shawn's in there."

"So? The last time I was in there, there were two shower stalls." JP sat across from Drake.

"No way am I going to shower with her."

JP snickered. "I never suggested that. All I did was point out there are two showers in there."

"Yeah, wouldn't she love to find me in there? She'd have a fit."

"She's not like that."

"Maybe not to you, but she sure is to me."

"Well, you have to admit, you deserve it."

"I'm just doing my job."

"And she's doing hers. Why can't you deal with it?"

"Women don't belong on boats." Drake stretched his

legs across the seat, hoping JP would drop the conversation.

"Hey," JP said, and Drake looked up.

Shawn had entered the galley, wearing a tiny tank top and a pair of shorts. She smiled at JP, while ignoring Drake.

"How's the finger?" JP asked.

"Fine." Shawn spoke without facing them as she selected a bandage from the first aid kit.

"Antibiotic ointment should be in there," JP said.

"Yeah, it's there," Shawn replied and opened the wrapper of the bandage.

The boat listed and the plastic box slid from the counter, spilling its contents on the floor.

When Shawn bent over to pick it up, Drake noticed how short her shorts were and cursed under his breath. He stood, took Shawn by the arm and pointed her at the booth. "Sit."

"What's your problem?" Shawn asked, standing her ground.

"Sit down." Drake nudged her toward the booth.

"What makes you think you can push me around? Don't you get enough fun from making my life as miserable as you can every chance you get?"

"Calm down," Drake said. "I was going to—"

"Going to nothing. I'm sick of you and your attitude."

Drake pointed toward the booth. "Sit down, damn it." He clenched and released his hands as he tried not to explode. He was trying to make up for his earlier mistake, but her response was annoying him.

"Then hit me and get it out of your system," Shawn said, with a pointed look at his fist. "You'll feel better, I'll feel better, and we can move on with life."

Drake noticed JP shaking his head in the corner of the galley.

"What?" Drake asked him. "I'm not going to hit her. I was going to clean her finger. We all know it's my fault it happened, so I'll fix it. Okay?"

JP opened the oven and Shawn sat down at the table without another word.

Drake slammed the first aid kit in front of her and went to the sink. After filling a bowl with hot tap water, he returned to the table, and sat across from her. "Let's see it."

Shawn unwrapped her hand and held it out. He took her by the wrist and turned it so he could see both sides then released her. He picked up the saltshaker and poured some into the water, then tested the salinity of the solution by dipping a finger in and tasting the saltwater. With a nod, he ordered her to put her hand in.

"I don't think so. That's going to sting."

Drake laughed. "You're worried about a little sting? You've stood up to me countless times, knowing I could beat the crap out of you. Probably believing I would. You've had a compound fracture and spent hours with bones sticking out of your arm. A crab tried to rip your finger off, and you're worried about the sting of salt in a cut?"

Shawn splashed her hand into the water.

"That's what I thought. All a person has to do is accuse you of being scared, and you jump in with both feet." He respected her nerve, even if he didn't like her.

Drake sorted and packed the contents of the first aid kit while Shawn soaked her hand. When the medical supplies were orderly, he set a tube of ointment on the table along with a bandage. "If you don't get it clean, it'll get infected."

"I think it's probably pretty clean. I washed it already and I spent fifteen minutes in the shower."

Drake lifted her hand from the water, set it on a pile of paper towels and took the bowl to the sink to empty. When he returned, Shawn was blotting her hand dry.

It wasn't dripping blood anymore, only oozing a little. He squeezed ointment onto his fingertip, surprised to see her hand shake when she held it toward him, and he wondered why she would tremble. Was she scared? Did he make her nervous enough for her hand to quiver?

Lana Voynich

"Why is it that the injury is never as bad as fixing it?" Shawn asked.

"I didn't realize it was." Drake held her hand steady and gently smeared the ointment into the cuts. "You're lucky. I've seen crabs take off fingers."

Shawn was silent.

Drake glanced up and noticed her face was pale. "You okay?"

Instead of responding, she dropped her forehead to the table.

Drake wiped the excess ointment from his finger. After folding a gauze pad, he wrapped it around her finger, taped it in place and set her hand gently on the table. He closed the kit and slid it aside. The lemony smell of her hair was subtle.

"All done," he said, and stood.

Shawn didn't react and Drake shook her shoulder. "Shawn?" Relief coursed through him when she lifted her head from the table.

"Done," Drake said.

"Oh. Did I pass out?"

"I guess. Is that normal for you?"

Shawn glanced at him, then lifted her hand and flexed her fingers the best she could with the bandage. After a few seconds, she met his gaze and said in a voice barely above a whisper, "Yeah. I don't know why."

Drake hung the kit back on the wall next to the fire extinguisher. "The longer you keep it dry, the faster it'll heal." He turned back to her. "I'll clean up after supper." He left the galley to take a shower before she had a chance to argue with him.

* * *

Some steam remained in the bathroom and the scent of Shawn's shampoo mingled with it. When Drake stepped into the shower, he was surprised to see she'd left her bottles and lotions next to his.

He turned the water as cold as he could stand. He

didn't want to be attracted to her.

The temperature of the water only shocked him for a few seconds. Images of Shawn played in his mind as he closed his eyes against the spray. Her arm reaching from the shower to grab the towel. Her legs sprawled across the bunk when he woke her from her nap the first day. The bare skin of her stomach when she raised her arms over her head. The flash in her eyes as she punched him. The sound of her laughter at JP's jokes.

The cold water wasn't doing anything to curb his attraction toward her. With a curse, he turned the knob to warm the temperature. It was stupid to take a cold shower on a crab boat in the Bering Sea. He forced his thoughts away from Shawn and grabbed the shampoo.

He squeezed some into his hand and started to lather up before he realized it was lemony. He grumbled, knowing instantly he had grabbed Shawn's shampoo. He rinsed it out and washed with his own shampoo. When he was done in the shower, he reached out of the stall, grabbed a towel and pulled it in.

He brought it to his face and smelled Shawn. "What is her problem? Does she have to leave her stuff all over the boat?" he growled.

"Sorry."

Drake jerked his head out of the towel and quickly wrapped it around his waist. "What are you doing here?" he asked, pushing the shower curtain to the side.

"I came in to get my stuff. Obviously, I got here too late."

"You don't have to pack it up. JP's stuff is in here. So is mine. And Dad's, too."

Shawn tipped her head to the side. "Then what's the big deal about my towel?"

"Nothing," Drake replied. He didn't want to tell her it wasn't the towel that bothered him. It was his growing attraction to her and the guilt he felt over his treatment of her. He wiped at the mirror with another towel and filled the sink with water. Rubbing shaving cream into his stubble, he looked at Shawn's reflection in the mirror. She was standing right inside the bathroom watching him.

He made eye contact with her. "You get your fill?" he asked, echoing her comment from the first day.

Shawn shook her head.

"You haven't?" Drake pulled the razor across his face.

"I wasn't checking you out."

Drake swished the razor in the water and held her gaze. "Then why are you watching me shave?"

Shawn finally spoke. "I don't know." She turned and pushed the curtain out of her way.

Drake smiled to himself. Maybe he affected her as much as she affected him. And if that was the case, he doubted she was any happier about it than he was. When he finished shaving, he dressed and hung her towel back on the rack.

Chapter Four

Shawn stretched in her bunk, feeling pretty good. An extra hour of rest was great, after only getting to sleep four or five out of every thirty hours. She saw JP napping in his bunk and rolled to face the wall, trying to understand her feelings. When she'd walked into the bathroom and heard Drake's voice, her first instinct was to retreat. Then he'd emerged from the shower with only a towel around his hips, and she'd lost her breath.

She couldn't remember what either of them had said or done, but the image of him was burned onto the backs of her eyelids. The droplets of water ran from his hair along the side of his neck and unchecked down his chest, finally stopping at the towel.

The steam in the room had carried the scent of his soap and, as ridiculous as it was, Shawn was jealous of her towel. His chest had a sprinkling of hair and then again right above the towel there was more. *He's your boss's son. Quit drooling. You have to work with him.*

She was more than physically attracted to him. His respect for Cap and JP had earned her admiration. His feeling of responsibility for her injury and his gentleness when tending her wound had made her reconsider her initial beliefs about him. It wouldn't be so hard to be nice to him now, knowing he could be kind.

Lifting her hand, she wondered why she couldn't see his fingerprints on her skin, as she could still feel where he'd touched her. Realizing she was curious what his hand would feel like if he'd touched her out of desire, rather than feeling obligated to dress her wound, Shawn forced the fantasy from her mind and slid from her bed. She glanced at the top two bunks, as she did every time she entered or exited the room, wondering if Drake was in one of them. He wasn't.

Thirsty, she went to the galley for a drink of water. The light over the sink was on, as always. Shawn moved to the sink, filled a mug, drank it and turned.

As she left the galley, she saw someone lying on the floor next to the booth. She knew it was Drake because JP was in his bunk, and Cap had his own stateroom where he'd be sleeping if he weren't captaining the boat. Shawn paused. She knew Drake chose to sleep on the floor rather than in the bunkroom because of her and it irritated her. He'd gone way past proving he didn't want her here.

The different thoughts running through her head surprised Shawn. She wanted to slip in the sleeping bag with him and wake him with her hands and mouth on his body, but she also wanted to kick him in the stomach and tell him how mad his behavior made her.

She stayed where she was. Either of her ideas would be satisfying, but they would make the remainder of the crab season even more uncomfortable.

She could see the waistband of his underwear from where he'd pushed the bag down and away from him. His left arm curled under his head and his right on his stomach, as his chest rose and fell slightly with each breath. When her gaze reached his face, smooth from the shave she'd witnessed earlier, she frowned.

She liked him better with his stubble. It was sexy and she wondered if she'd be able to control herself if he wasn't clean-shaven right now. She blinked, amazed at her thoughts. It didn't matter if he was sporting a full beard; she wasn't going to crawl in the sleeping bag with him. She heard a rustle of movement and shifted her gaze to his eyes. They were still closed. She exhaled and turned to leave, not needing any more images of him tormenting her every time she closed her eyes.

She gasped when she saw a figure against the wall on

the other side of the hallway. "JP," she whispered. "What are you doing?"

"I'm on wheel watch tonight," he said as he entered the galley.

"Wheel watch?"

"Yeah, so Cap can get some sleep."

Shawn peeked at Drake again. "I wondered if Cap ever slept."

"Drake and I take turns." JP filled a mug from the coffee pot. "Want to keep me company?"

Shawn considered it, then shook her head. "I don't think so."

"I won't mention anything about you staring at Drake, if that's what's stopping you."

* * *

Shawn shushed JP and motioned toward the wheelhouse as Drake shifted in his sleep.

JP led the way up the stairs. Shawn knew she'd have to deal with her feelings for Drake, which had shifted from dislike to admiration in the amount of time it took him to bandage her finger, so it might as well be now.

"You brought backup?" Cap teased JP when they entered the wheelhouse.

"I was curious," Shawn replied, not about to admit how JP had blackmailed her into joining him.

"Not much to see but a lot of darkness," Cap responded. He gave JP a quick rundown of where they were headed before he left the wheelhouse.

JP settled into the captain's chair and Shawn perched in the other seat, looking around, and avoiding JP's gaze. The four sides of the room were glass and the room was dark, except for the glow of the various screens and monitors. The chatter over the radio was a comfortable reminder they weren't the last people in the world. With a sigh, Shawn focused her attention on JP.

JP checked a few readings and turned to Shawn. "How much of this do you know?"

"Not enough to captain a boat."

"Is that why you're here? To learn to captain?"

"No, I wanted to see if it was like I remembered."

"And?"

"Some things are the same. Others are different."

"Like everything in life."

Shawn remained quiet.

"What's different?" JP asked.

"Grandpa's not here. It's not his boat."

"Nope. But it's a good boat and we've got a great crew."

Shawn remained silent. She couldn't disagree with him about the crew even though it had been difficult to tolerate Drake's presence until a few hours ago.

"You're a good deckhand," JP said.

Shawn knew she was doing the best she could, but had never been comfortable with praise so ignored his compliment and said, "I try."

"So, what's the same?"

Shawn turned toward the window, looking at the reflections from the monitors as she formulated a response. "The hard work, the ache in my muscles."

They were both silent a while. After about fifteen minutes, she spoke again. "I don't know what it is about him."

Shawn was grateful JP continued staring straight ahead. She didn't know if she'd be able to keep talking if he faced her. "One minute I want to smack him and the next I find myself wanting to... I don't know."

"He probably feels the same way."

"Why do you say that?"

"The way he looks at you sometimes."

Shawn drew back in the seat, surprised by JP's comment. She harrumphed and said, "All I am to him is a pain in the ass."

"He's got a hard time trusting women. Cut him a little slack."

Shawn considered asking why Drake couldn't trust women, but didn't. She already knew enough to make it hard not to be attracted to him. She didn't want to be hurt and humiliated by a man again. She turned away. "Consider it done." After a few more minutes of silence, she stood. "I think I'm going to bed."

"Don't get cranky. I was trying to explain him to you."

"I'm not cranky. I think he's attractive, but I'm not interested in him the way you seem to think I am."

"I don't think anything. I've seen him give you the same looks you were giving him tonight. And I know he's a nice guy."

"I work with him. I'm not going to date him."

JP raised his hands in a placating manner. "I never said you should."

"I'm going to bed before my foot gets wedged any further in my mouth." Shawn smiled to show she wasn't angry and started down to the galley.

"He's a pretty sound sleeper. Feel free to ogle him on your way," JP teased as she descended.

* * *

The lights were on, revealing Drake had moved from the floor to the table. When he looked up, Shawn raised her chin a fraction of an inch. Drake remained silent and dropped his gaze to the magazine in front of him on the table.

"Can I talk to you for a minute?" Shawn asked.

Drake grunted.

"Do you try to be annoying or is it something that comes to you naturally?" Shawn spoke before thinking.

Drake looked up and the left half of his mouth curled into a smile.

"I want to apologize," Shawn said.

"For?"

"For punching you." Shawn took deep breath and Drake turned his attention back to the magazine.

"Well, to be honest, I was going to apologize, but every time I talk to you, I want to punch you all over again."

Drake nodded without looking up. "I've been told that before."

Shawn flipped his magazine shut. Drake scowled to show his annoyance.

Shawn bit her lip then said, "I'm tired of this. I apologize for hitting you. Do you think we can be civil?"

"Maybe." Drake shifted on the bench. "Look, I don't know what you expect, but I'm treating you like I treat everyone else."

"Liar. You respect JP and you haven't shown me an iota of respect."

"I've known JP my entire life. Besides, you're not here to make friends. You're here to make a pile of money so you can go back home and tell your friends about your big adventure."

Shawn threw her hands up in exasperation. "You really think that's the kind of person I am?"

Drake opened the magazine. "Why does it matter? I don't understand why you care so much about what someone you don't even like thinks."

Shawn faltered, realizing he was right. She didn't know why she cared. Normally, other people's opinions of her didn't matter. Without answering the question, she forged ahead. "I don't like you because you're full of preconceived ideas about me that aren't correct."

"Really?"

"Yeah."

"How do you know they're not?"

"Because you treat me like I'm the scum of the Earth and I'm not that bad."

"You're in your mid to late-twenties. You don't know what you want from life. You came to Alaska because you're running away from something and you don't get along with your parents." Drake's smile was cold as he asked, "How close am I?"

Shawn met his gaze, trying to hide her surprise at the accuracy of his statements. "How do you figure?"

"You're younger than me, but you've been in the

Coast Guard so you're between twenty-two and thirty-one. If you knew what you wanted from life, you'd be doing it already. And you haven't mentioned your family at all. On top of that, you don't trust any of us on *The KayLeigh*.

"You're wrong."

"Really?"

"I trust you."

"Me? Or the entire crew?"

"Both."

"Why?"

"You know your job and you do it well. You won't let me get hurt even if you want to throw me overboard." Her voice grew quieter as she looked away. "You're probably even a nice guy. You just don't like me." She raised her eyes back to his. "I'm okay with that. I don't have to like you to trust you. I wish you felt the same way."

"Why do I get the impression you're keeping something from us?"

Shifting her gaze from his again, she countered, "Does my entire life need to be an open book?"

"No."

"I'll answer any question you ask if you'll tell me why you hate me."

Drake closed the magazine.

Shawn was surprised when he said, "Any question?"

"Yeah. And you can't say women on boats bring bad luck."

"What if that's the only reason I have?"

"Then you're stupider than I thought," Shawn replied with a smile to take the edge from her words.

"Why are you here?"

Shawn turned to the sink to get a drink of water. When she turned back, Drake was watching her. The expression on his face told her he expected her to avoid the question. She rubbed the scar on her arm and took a deep breath. "Do you want the short version or the whole drawn out ordeal?"

"The truth."

"I wanted to get away from my life so I could sort

some stuff out."

Drake tipped his head to the side, and she spoke in a rush. She didn't expect any sympathy from him, but was tired of hiding the truth. "The guy I was engaged to eloped with my best friend. My parents don't know and I didn't want to deal with it. I came back to Alaska because it was the furthest I could get from all of them and the last place they'll look for me."

"Sounds like fun."

"No, it's not," Shawn said, and wrapped her arms around her waist.

"That pretty much explains all of my preconceived ideas. And I think they were pretty accurate."

"I don't need to hear how much smarter you are than me. I should have known you'd back out of the deal."

"I didn't back out. I don't think you want to hear it."

Shawn held his gaze.

"JP's married."

"What in the world does that have to do with me?"

"I don't respect anyone who doesn't respect marriage."

"You can't be serious. We sleep in the same bunkroom. I'm not in love with him." Shawn laughed humorlessly at the thought of having an affair with JP just as JP walked into the galley.

"What's so funny?" JP asked as he refilled his coffee mug from the pot.

Shawn glanced at Drake, tempted to tell JP how stupid his friend was acting but decided against it. She faced JP and said, "Nothing. Drake made a joke."

* * *

After lying in her bunk for a couple of hours, Shawn fell asleep but couldn't stay that way. She felt like she'd slept too much, which was ridiculous since she'd only had six hours of sleep in the past thirty, but her body had become accustomed to four hours of sleep. Worried if she started sleeping more, she'd struggle when they started crabbing again, she rolled out of her bunk and went to the galley.

Relieved it was empty, she settled into the booth with a deck of cards. Dealing out a game of solitaire, she tried not to think about Drake. *Don't I have enough to worry about without adding him to the mix?*

Angry with herself for dwelling on what JP had said about Drake watching her, Shawn shook her head. Nothing was going to happen. It didn't matter how he did or didn't look at her. She would never date someone so adamant she didn't belong somewhere she chose to be. It was too much like her parents.

Sometimes it seemed the only thing she'd done in her life to meet her parent's approval was getting engaged to Ethan. From the moment they met him, they'd done everything they could to welcome him into the family.

"Do you ever sleep?"

Shawn jumped at Drake's voice. She looked up and asked, "Do you?"

"Yeah, sometimes." He turned to the stove. After fixing a cup of tea, he sat down across from her.

"I can't seem to sleep," Shawn said, gathering the cards from her forgotten game of solitaire.

"It takes me a few weeks to get back to sleeping a full night."

Shawn stared at Drake in wonder.

"What?" he asked, bringing his mug to his mouth.

"Are we actually having a conversation?"

"If that's what you want to call it."

Shawn relaxed into the booth, thinking how his pleasant demeanor made her feelings even more awkward.

"It sucks about that guy and your friend."

Talking about Ethan would mean she had to think about him and she didn't want to do that, so she spoke in a joking manner, certain Drake had realized the ridiculousness of his accusation. "Did you ask JP?"

"Ask JP what?"

"If we're having an affair."

"No, it's none of my business."

"It wasn't any of your business earlier, either. That didn't stop you from deciding you hate me because of it."

"Grow up." Drake stood, dumped the remainder of his tea down the sink drain and faced her.

Taken aback, Shawn repeated his words. "Grow up?"

"Quit feeling sorry for yourself. No one said that I hate you."

"No one had to say it. It's obvious."

"What's the big deal? You don't like me."

"That's because you're constantly being a jerk."

"And you're always so pleasant to be around."

Shawn stood; her neck was starting to ache from looking up at him. "How about you? What mature person sleeps on the floor because he doesn't want to share a room with a woman?"

"How does where I sleep have any impact on you?"

"I think it's stupid."

"I think it's stupid to run away from your problems and end up on a crab boat."

"Why? What is wrong with ending up on a crab boat?"

"You're a woman. How many times do I have to point that out?" Drake raked his hand through his hair.

"Get over it. Don't you think I realize I'm a woman every time I go to the bathroom or put on a bra?"

Drake stared at her, apparently speechless.

"What?" Shawn demanded.

"I wasn't saying you didn't know. I was saying—"

"Yeah, yeah, yeah. Women don't belong on boats. I got it. How could I possibly forget everything comes back to that?" Shawn stormed out of the galley, frustrated they were back to the same point when she thought they'd moved past it.

* * *

"We're docking," JP said as he walked into the bunkroom, rubbing his wet hair with a towel, forty-five minutes after Shawn left the galley.

"And?" Shawn asked, curt due to her frustration toward Drake.

"You've got a few hours, if you need anything."

"Like what?"

"Stock up on chocolate milk? Call home?" JP pulled on an insulated flannel shirt. "Do laundry?" He crammed his clothes into a garbage bag.

"Clean clothes sound great." Shawn stuffed her dirty laundry into her bag and turned to JP. "Show me the way."

After leaving the boat, JP led her to a laundromat and they quickly took over a pair of washing machines.

"I've got about a load and a half. You?" Shawn asked, dumping her clothes into a washer.

"About the same."

"Throw your half load in with mine." Shawn bought a box of detergent from the vending machine and dumped some into the three washers. When Drake stepped into the laundromat and set a duffel bag on the washer next to hers, Shawn offered him the box of detergent. She was feeding quarters to the washers when Drake spoke.

"We'll be here four to five hours. They're short-handed at the processor."

JP went to the change machine, dropped some quarters on the counter, then went to the pay phone in the back corner away from the seats. Shawn pulled a worn book from her pack and opened it as she watched Drake from the corner of her eye. When he filled one washer and started to drop clothes into the next one, she said, "The middle one isn't full. You might as well throw yours in there if you don't have a lot left."

Drake transferred his clothes into the shared washer and sorted through the stack of magazines on the windowsill next to Shawn.

JP turned his back to them and was still on the phone when the washers finished. Shawn shifted the clothes to the dryers and sat as Drake stood to move his load. She stretched her legs to prop them on a washing machine, meeting Drake's gaze and holding it. When he grinned, Shawn smiled back.

Drake stood against the washer she was using as a footstool. When she felt the heat from his leg on her leg, she dropped her feet and shifted to look out the window. After a few minutes of silence, she turned back toward Drake. "Want to show me Dutch Harbor?" she asked, expecting him to decline.

She was shocked when he said, "Yeah, sure." He glanced at the time left on the dryers and picked up some quarters. "Let's feed these first."

Shawn returned to the dryers and opened the first one in line to remove the dry clothes, noticing a pair of long underwear, a bra, and a pair of boxers in her hand. Drake pulled out a handful of bikini panties and long underwear from the next dryer and dropped them in the basket. Shawn divided the remaining damp clothes between the dryers and restarted them before she dumped the basket on the counter and started folding.

"You don't have to fold my laundry," Drake said, and picked some of his belongings from the pile.

"I know I don't have to, but I don't mind. Besides, I don't know what's yours and what's JP's." Shawn quickly worked her way through the t-shirts and underwear on the table. She felt her face grow warm each time one of her undergarments appeared in the pile, but dropped them into her open pack. When the laundry was folded, she looked at Drake. "Ready?"

"For?"

"The tour," she replied. "Or are you going to back out?"

"Nope. Just wondering if we were thinking the same thing."

"And?"

"We were."

* * *

Shawn followed Drake outside after they put on their jackets. They wandered a few blocks without speaking, until Drake blurted, "I'm sorry for what I said."

"What did you say?"

"I said I'm sorry for what I said."

"I heard you. But, what are you apologizing for? I'd hate to forgive you for something you didn't apologize for."

Drake cleared his throat and said, "About you and JP. Like you said, it's none of my business."

"No, it isn't. But there's nothing going on."

Drake turned left.

Shawn followed him and when they walked past a grocery store, she pointed through the window at the pay phone. "Do you mind?" She owed her parents a call. She hadn't talked to them in a couple weeks, and they didn't know she'd left Seattle. Or that Ethan and Addi had eloped.

"No, I can get some more tea." Drake pulled a handful of change from his pocket and offered it to her.

After checking her pockets and coming up empty, Shawn plucked a quarter from his hand. "Thanks."

Drake continued into the store.

Shawn inserted the quarter into the pay phone and dialed. As the phone rang, she looked around the entrance of the store. Other than the never-brightening-past-gray light, it was like any other grocery store. Dirty tiles on the floor with years of crud ground into the seams. Metal grocery carts lined up, waiting their turn. Gumball machines and one of those stuffed animal cranes were next to the phone.

Shawn waited for the operator to connect the call. She focused on a purple cow in the crane and heard her mother accept the charges for the collect call.

"Shawn Marie, where are you? We've been worried sick." The voice moved away from the phone. "I don't know, Bill. She's not answering." Her mom grew louder as she moved her mouth closer to the receiver. "Why isn't anyone answering their phone out there? I even called Ethan and he won't answer, either."

Shawn pressed her forehead against the cool glass of the crane and let her mother's voice wash through her, feeling relief and love. "Hi, Mom. How are you?"

"Worried sick. What's going on?" Deb didn't even give her a chance to answer before asking another question. "Why are you calling collect?"

The happiness at hearing her mother's voice was quickly replaced with the dread of telling her what had happened. "I'm not at home and I don't have my calling card with me."

"Are you okay?"

"There have been some changes to the wedding plans."

"You eloped? How could you? You know how much I was looking forward to your wedding."

"No, Mom. We didn't elope; Ethan did." Shawn took a deep breath and forced herself to say, "With Addi." She bowed her head and swiped at her eyes. *It shouldn't hurt this much.*

"What? But that doesn't make any sense."

"I know, Mom." Shawn looked up when Drake approached and offered her a bottle of chocolate milk. "Thanks," she mouthed, finger up. "I'll be another minute." She took the milk and set it on the ledge next to the phone book.

"No rush," he responded with a look of concern.

Unable to meet his gaze, Shawn focused on her dirty shoes. She'd been happy to leave her boots on the boat and wear her old running shoes for the short trek into town.

"Who's that? What's going on?" Deb questioned.

"It's Drake. I have to go, Mom."

"What? Who's Drake? Are you sleeping with him? Is he the reason Ethan married someone else?"

"I have to get back to work." Shawn avoided the question.

"Where are you working?"

For some reason, it hurt even to hear her mother's voice. Shawn swallowed the lump in her throat and spoke. "A crab boat." She took a deep breath and continued. "I'm sorry I worried you. I wasn't thinking clearly when I left."

"What?"

Shawn laughed at the shock in Deb's voice. It was exactly as Shawn had expected.

"Come home, honey, and we'll get everything sorted out."

"I can't afford to. Ethan used my savings to pay for his wedding."

Shawn heard Drake curse and turned from him to concentrate on calming her mother down. "Mom, I'm not coming to Minnesota right now. I'll visit when I'm done fishing and I'll explain everything then. I promise."

"Where are you? Your father and I will come to you."

Shawn felt defeated. This was why she hadn't wanted to call. Her mom didn't like to let Shawn figure things out on her own. "Right now I'm in Dutch Harbor, but we're leaving soon."

"Where?"

"Alaska, Mom." Shawn smiled at her mother's gasp of surprise.

"When will you be back?"

"I don't know."

"Will you be returning to Dutch Harbor?"

"I don't know. I got on the boat in Kodiak. I assume that's where we'll be docking when we're done." Shawn glanced at Drake and tried to cut off the rest of the questions she knew her mother had by speaking in a rush. "Mom, I have to go. I need to finish my laundry and get back to the boat before it leaves. I love you. Tell Dad I said 'hi'." Shawn hung up the phone and slumped against the wall, raising both hands to rub her now throbbing temples.

After a few moments, she straightened, dropped her hands from her head, grabbed the bottle of milk and left the store, assuming Drake would follow her. He fell into step next to her and didn't say anything until she turned toward him and asked, "How long until we leave?"

He glanced at his watch. "An hour or so."

"Can I borrow your watch?"

"Sure," he said, and handed it to her after unfastening

it from his wrist. "Why?"

"I want to go for a run." Shawn fastened the watch on the smallest setting and pushed it up her forearm until it stayed in place.

"A what?"

She smiled at his expression. "A run," she repeated.

"Why? Nobody's chasing you."

"No one that you can see," she replied, tucking the bottle of milk into her jacket pocket. She unzipped the jacket and held it toward him. "Can you leave this at the laundromat with my pack?"

"I can take it back to the boat, along with your laundry if you want to meet us there."

"Really? You wouldn't mind?"

"No, it's fine."

Shawn kissed him on the cheek without thinking, then pulled back, surprised and embarrassed at her reaction to his kindness. "Thanks. I really appreciate it," she said and jogged away from him.

"You're even crazier than I thought," he called after her as she loped down the sidewalk. When she turned the corner at the end of the block, she saw he was still standing there, watching her.

Shawn ran toward the harbor and along the coast, settling into her normal pace and enjoying the scenery and the feel of freedom. When she was thirty minutes from where she'd started, she turned around and sprinted back.

When she reached the town limits, she slowed to a jog, pulled off her sweatshirt, and tied it around her waist, welcoming the cool air on her bare arms as she retraced the route she'd taken with Drake from the laundromat.

She rounded the corner as JP and Drake emerged, carrying three bags of laundry and her jacket. Shawn slid to a stop and said, "Right on time."

"No way," JP said. "Drake was serious? You really went for a run?"

Shawn pulled her sweatshirt back on over her t-shirt and took her coat and pack from Drake. "Thanks," she said, and slung the pack over her shoulder.

JP walked away, scratching his head while Drake kept pace beside Shawn. She met his gaze and whispered, "What's with him?"

"No idea. Must be thinking about something Celia said."

Shawn pulled the bottle of milk from her coat pocket and opened it.

"You okay?" Drake asked when she didn't speak.

"Probably not okay, but better anyway. Running usually makes life better." She finished the chocolate milk and dropped the bottle in a trashcan as she passed it. "Thanks again for the milk."

Drake nodded in acknowledgment of her gratitude and said, "Where'd you go?"

"I ran." Shawn was amazed at how well they were getting along. It seemed surreal to be talking and walking with Drake instead of JP. "I went out of town past a restaurant, and then ran along the shore for a ways."

"So you ran for a couple miles?"

Shawn adjusted her bag and said, "I guess so."

"You run a lot?"

"A couple times a day, when I can. It's a good stress reliever."

"How far?" Drake asked as they turned onto the dock next to the processor.

"Between four and five miles."

"No wonder you're so hard to get along with."

Shawn's step faltered. She thought they were getting along and now this. She glanced over at him. "What?" she asked, and cocked her head to the side.

"You have enough stress in your life to need to run five miles a day?"

Shawn considered his question for a second, then said, "Some days. Sometimes I run just to run."

"Yet, you're trapped on an eighty-two foot boat with three guys and no place to run. How do you cope?"

She realized Drake was teasing her, and said, "I don't."

"I've noticed."

"I take it out on the people around me."

"I suppose you make poor defenseless, undeserving people pay for your stress."

Shawn stepped onto *The KayLeigh* and nodded at him.

Once the boat was away from the dock and the traffic of the harbor, she carried her gear into the bunkroom and saw JP lying on his bunk staring at the underside of the mattress above him. "You okay?"

He grunted.

"Was that an answer? Or are you choking to death?"

JP smiled half-heartedly. "I'm fine."

"You sure?"

"Just some family stuff."

"Anything I can do to help?"

"I doubt it."

Shawn sat on the edge of his bunk and patted his arm with a caring smile. "Give me a shot."

"It's nothing."

"You're my friend. Let me help."

JP shook his head. "Don't wanna talk about it right now."

"I can understand that. If you change your mind, you know where to find me."

JP sat up on the edge of his bunk and said in a low voice. "I'm thinking of quitting."

Confused, Shawn asked, "Quitting what?"

"This." JP waved his hand to indicate the room, the boat.

"Why?"

After looking around the room to make sure they were alone, JP spoke softly. "This can't go any further than your ears.'

"I'm good at keeping secrets."

"Celia is upset I'm never home. I miss her and Preston. I think it might be time for me to grow up. Time to be a real husband and a dad to our little girl."

JP pulled a photo from the wall and handed it to Shawn.

Gently, she accepted it. JP was sitting on a chair, arms

around a beautiful blonde who held a little girl. All three were happy.

"What's up?" Drake pushed aside the curtain and entered the room.

"Nothing much." Shawn handed the photo back. "JP was showing me a picture of Preston. She's a cutie."

Drake grinned. "Of course she is. She's my goddaughter."

JP had to decide what was best for his family; he also had the weight of knowing Drake would be hurt if he left. Shawn didn't envy him his decision.

Shawn glanced down at her arm and noticed Drake's watch was still there. She took it off and handed it to him. "Thanks," she said and stood.

"No problem." Drake backed out of the way to let Shawn pass him into the hallway. Shawn noticed he smiled, but her thoughts were on JP's dilemma instead of her own at the moment.

* * *

Shawn dug a bucket and cleaning supplies from the closet and carried them into the head. She had always enjoyed cleaning bathrooms. She liked seeing her progress and prided herself on making a bathroom sparkle.

While she scrubbed the sink she replayed the conversation with her mother in her head. It seemed just as bad the second time around. She shouldn't have called, but she knew her parents would be worried about her. She definitely shouldn't have told her mother where she was.

Shawn's parents were the first of their families to use their brains rather than their backs to earn a living. They couldn't understand physical labor was something Shawn enjoyed. Aching muscles at the end of the day made Shawn feel she'd accomplished something. She loved being exhausted when she went to bed on *The KayLeigh*.

Shawn was shocked at her reaction to Drake's expression when he overheard that Ethan had taken her money. She wanted to cry on his shoulder while he comforted her. Never wanting anyone to take care of her before, Shawn was amazed Drake could make her feel so out of character.

Shawn shook her thoughts from her head and looked around the bathroom. She'd scrubbed the sink, both shower stalls and the toilet. All that was left was mopping. She filled the bucket with water and swished the mop around the floor, focusing on the cleaning instead of Drake, Ethan and her mother. When she was done, she smiled.

* * *

A few hours after they left the processor, Shawn entered the galley as Drake stepped in from the deck. She swallowed hard but refused to miss supper due to her inability to deal with her feelings for him.

"Right on time," JP said, as Drake settled into the booth with his cup of tea.

"Need any help?" Shawn offered.

JP set a platter of pot roast on the table. "Everything is done. Just eat."

Shawn slid into the booth across from Drake and began to eat as Cap and JP joined them at the table.

Within minutes, the four of them were talking and joking. It was the most pleasant meal Shawn had shared with them. Toward the end of dinner, Shawn asked, "So Cap, how'd the boat get her name?"

"Kay Leigh is my daughter's name," Cap said quietly.

"I didn't know you had a daughter." Shawn glanced at Drake. "Does she know what a chauvinist you are?"

JP nudged Shawn's leg with his and shook his head.

Shawn looked at Drake and saw anger on his face.

"Kay died when she was three." Cap said, standing. "Thanks for another great meal, JP."

Shawn looked at Drake. "I'm sorry. I didn't know."

"Yeah." Drake stormed out of the galley.

"It's a bit of a sensitive topic for Drake." JP finished his meal and slid out of the booth.

"Really? I'd never have guessed." Shawn narrowed her eyes at JP's statement.

"That's right; I forgot how observant you are."

"Funny."

"Calm down. I'll tell you about it while we clean up."

"What do you mean while we clean up? You cooked."

"Yeah, but cleaning up is the time to gossip. I learned that from my mom and my sisters. They always gabbed when they did the dishes. Unless I was in the room."

"And you felt left out?" Shawn teased.

"Not really." JP slid out of the booth and carried empty dishes to the sink. "Don't worry. I don't plan on helping much."

Shawn laughed and filled the sink with water.

"Drake's mom left when he was five. She took Kay with her and Drake never saw her again."

"Her, Kay? Or her, his mom?"

"Neither. He told me once that his mom wanted to see him when he was about fifteen and he'd refused to go. Cap tried to make him and he threatened to run away."

"Where would he have gone?"

"That's probably why Cap backed down; he didn't have any idea where Drake would go, either."

"What happened to his sister?"

"She got sick. I think it was pneumonia and his mom didn't take her to the doctor soon enough. I'm not sure exactly how it happened, but I know Drake blames his mother for Kay's death. That's why he won't see her. Plus the fact she left him here."

"I barely know him and I know he wouldn't be happy anywhere else."

"It's entirely possible his mom knew that even when he was five. I don't know. All I've ever heard was Drake's side. And of course the gossip around town."

Shawn wiped her hands on a towel and faced JP, resting a hip against the counter. "What kind of gossip?"

"The normal stuff, like she was cheating on Cap and left with some guy... A guy who didn't like Drake so she left him with Cap."

"That's normal gossip? I'd hate to hear what you call 'big news'."

"It's what you hear whenever someone disappears. No one seems to know the real story other than Cap and her. It's none of my business, so I've never tried to learn more about it."

"Is that why Drake hates women?"

"I know it's hard to believe but Drake doesn't hate women. He just doesn't trust them."

"Because of his mom?"

"That's my guess. Again, I've never asked."

"Men." Shawn shook her head. "Don't you think it's your business when something's bothering your friend?"

"Is it any of my business you're running away from something? Is it any of your business I'm trying to decide my future?"

"I suppose a little. And what do you mean I'm running away from something?"

"I assumed you were, but like we both said, it's none of my business."

"Right. But I also admit I feel better knowing someone cares. Even if I don't feel like telling you what I'm running from."

"Oh? So, I'm right?"

"Yeah. You're right, but I don't want to talk about it."

"See, as a man, I'm okay with that. I assume you know I'd listen if you wanted to tell me, but I'm not going to ask again. I'm going to mind my own business."

"For some reason, I doubt that."

"Doubt what?"

"That you'll mind your own business. You don't seem like that kind of guy."

"I haven't asked you why you're hiding out on a crab boat in the Bering Sea. That's minding my own business, isn't it?"

"I swear it's nothing against you. I don't want to think about it, and it's kind of hard not to think about if I have to explain it to someone."

"It's cool, honest."

"Yet, I nagged you until you told me what was bothering you."

"That's the difference between us. It's not a problem. If you need to talk, I'm here. If you want someone to get drunk with, I can do that, too." He grinned. "Of course, we won't be able to do that until we're done with the crabs."

Shawn looked up as Drake returned to the galley.

"Can I talk to you?" Drake said over his shoulder as he set the teapot on the stove.

"Me or JP?" Shawn asked.

"You."

JP stood and spoke as he left the room. "Only say nice things about me."

"What?" Drake asked.

"Since you're obviously going to talk about me, make sure you only say nice things."

"Yeah, right." Drake chuckled, and turned toward Shawn.

Shawn rolled the cup between her palms until she realized she was fidgeting, which Drake might view as nervousness. She set the mug on the table, while she waited for Drake to speak.

"What's up?" she asked, when she couldn't stand the silence any more.

"Sorry. What you said shouldn't have upset me so much."

Shawn felt his apology was unnecessary. "I shouldn't have said it."

"How could you have known?" Drake stood when the teapot whistled. "Neither of us seem to have the greatest family story, huh?"

Shawn looked down. "I guess life isn't perfect for anyone." She frowned as she recalled the conversation with her mom again.

"What's the worst thing your parents ever did to you?" Drake asked.

Shawn watched him fill his mug with water, drop in a

tea bag, and fix another mug. He set one across from her, taking her empty cup to the sink and rinsing it.

"You want to compare war stories?" she asked.

"Just making conversation," he admitted, sliding into the booth across from her.

Shawn swallowed and tipped her head to the side as she looked at him. She considered telling him how her parents viewed manual laborers, how her grandfather had owned a fishing boat, and how they'd reacted when they learned she was in Alaska when she was fifteen. She decided to keep it to herself, knowing he'd be upset when he learned of *Poseidon* and suspecting he'd be insulted by her family's treatment of the working class. "Why? I don't really want to talk about my family."

Drake sipped his tea. "Why not? You're going to think about it whether you talk about it or not. That's what everyone's been telling me for the past twenty-five years."

"Were they right? Do you think about it even though you didn't talk about it?"

After a moment of silence, Drake nodded. "Yeah. Not all the time, but it's usually in the back of my head."

"What happened twenty-five years ago?" Shawn wrapped her hands around the warm mug and lifted it to her mouth to sip.

Drake met her gaze. "My mom took my little sister and left me and Dad."

"I'm sorry."

"Why are you sorry? You didn't have anything to do with it."

"I brought it up."

Drake leaned against the wall with his legs stretched in front of him across the bench. "It's always there. Even when no one brings it up."

Shawn took another swallow of her tea. "This is good. What is it?"

"Mango."

Eyes wide, Shawn chuckled. "That's the last thing I thought you'd drink."

"Really? Why's that?"

"I don't know. You're such a... Such a man. You seem like the type to drink whiskey straight and coffee, strong and black."

A look of puzzlement crossed his face. "Was that an insult?"

"No. Why would you ask that?"

"I'm 'such a man'?"

Shawn felt her face grow warm as she realized what she'd said. And meant. How was she going to explain away her statement without incriminating herself? "I meant you seem like a very masculine guy. The type who likes football, hockey and boxing. No time for golf or any of the more genteel things in life."

Drake laughed. "You're right. I don't have any desire to chase a ball around a pasture or to listen to opera, but I like tea."

"And I like chocolate milk." Shawn took another sip. "But this is good, too." She shifted in her seat to mirror his position. She was more comfortable around him, but it didn't mean she was attracted to him. Although that would be a deathblow to her mother and father. Shawn let out a snort of laughter and quickly covered her mouth with her hand.

"What's so funny?" Drake asked.

"I was thinking about how my parents would react to you."

"What do you mean?"

"The worst thing my parents ever did was not understand me. They worked hard so they didn't have to perform manual labor to survive. And they've never understood that I like my muscles to ache when I go to bed; it makes me feel I've done something worthwhile.

"My parents would look down on you, because you're a fisherman. The same as they looked down on me for joining the Coast Guard."

Drake waited without speaking.

"Ethan, my fiancé... Ex-fiancé, that is, recently finished his residency in pediatrics and my parents were ecstatic when I brought him home. They thought I'd finally realized how great it was to rely on my mind. They were hoping he'd talk some sense into me and convince me to pursue a more intellectual career." Shawn paused to drink some more tea and didn't look at Drake when she continued.

"My mother heard me talking to you and she asked if I was sleeping with you. She's a bit crass about some things."

"And you laughed a minute ago because you were thinking how she'd react if you brought me home?"

"Yeah, I guess. Not that I was planning on bringing you home. You're lucky enough you'll never have to meet my parents."

They were both silent for a bit, then Drake spoke.

"Why do you do that?"

"Do what?"

"Rub your arm."

Shawn looked down and saw she was rubbing the scar on her arm like she could erase it with enough pressure. "I don't know. A nervous twitch I guess."

"So you're nervous?"

"No, not really. More like apprehensive."

"Why?"

She answered cautiously. "Because now you know enough to use it against me."

"And we all know what a jerk I am."

Shawn smiled apologetically. "I shouldn't have said that, either."

"I didn't know you had."

"I should shut up before I get myself in trouble."

"I'm curious why you told me. You didn't have to. You could have told me to mind my own business."

"I already tried that today with JP."

"You did?"

"Yeah."

"And yet you told me?"

"Trust me; I'm even more surprised than you are. I have no idea why I told you."

"Must be my chauvinism that wore you down."

Shawn realized he was teasing her again. "Yeah, that must be it." She slid out of the booth and crossed to the sink to rinse her cup. "Thanks for the tea."

"One more thing."

"What's that?"

"Was I right? Do you think about it even when you don't talk about it?"

Shawn nodded.

* * *

Shawn rolled over in her bunk and opened her eyes. The light was on in the hall and something was hanging from the top bunk. She assumed it was the sleeve of a sweatshirt and reached up to bat it out of the way as she rose. She was shocked to feel human flesh.

She jerked her hand back. JP was asleep in his bunk; she could hear him snoring. Cap slept in his stateroom off of the wheelhouse. That meant Drake must be in the bunk above her. She pulled her legs back into her bunk and lay down. Drake was sleeping in the same room as her. What did it mean?

She got out of the bunk. *It probably means he's tired of sleeping on the galley floor* Shawn thought and left the room.

When Shawn returned from the head, and her eyes adjusted to the dimness, she turned her attention to Drake. He was sprawled across the bunk on his stomach, with his face turned toward the room. His head rested on his arm and his sleeping bag was pushed down around his hips, revealing his back.

Shawn wanted to touch him as she caressed his bare skin with her eyes. The side of his face and his neck, corded with tendons and muscles. His long fingers curled into the mattress. His arms and shoulders, relaxed completely. Over his back and down to his waist where the dark nylon of his sleeping bag covered him. She considered tugging on the sleeping bag, to reveal more of him. Amazed at her thoughts, Shawn moved forward.

If Drake opened his eyes, Shawn would be all he saw.

She wondered what his reaction would be to such an awakening. When he groaned, Shawn stepped back, holding her breath until he was quiet again. He rolled on to his back and kicked his legs free of the covers. She couldn't tell if he was wearing boxers or briefs, but that was the only covered part of his body.

Shawn forced herself into her bunk. If she looked at him much longer, she might embarrass herself with her actions. She lay on her back and pulled her sleeping bag over her. She heard Drake shifting in the berth above her and looked up at the bunk, wishing she could see through it before closing her eyes and remembering what she'd seen.

* * *

Drake opened his eyes when he heard Shawn settle into her bunk. He'd been awake when she swatted his leg, but he hadn't moved because he was curious what she'd do when she noticed his presence. He was surprised that she stopped right in front of him. He could smell her shampoo and even feel her breath on his face when she exhaled.

He'd peeked through slitted eyelids when he shifted on the bed and saw she was gazing at him like she wanted to join him in the bunk. It might have been underhanded and sneaky of him to roll over and purposely push the blankets further from his body, knowing she was staring at him, but it seemed warmer in the room when she was standing so close.

Drake had felt uncomfortable while she looked at him, but he couldn't complain because he'd done the same earlier. He'd waited until JP was asleep, so he didn't have to explain himself as he stood next to the bunks gazing at her. She'd been covered by her sleeping bag with only her head and scarred arm exposed.

It was all he could do to keep from touching her, to see if her hair was as silky as it looked. To trace the scar with his finger, and feel what she felt when she rubbed it.

He'd reached toward her, intending to touch the lock of hair on her pillow. But when she mumbled and shifted in her sleep, he jerked his hand back, and hoisted himself into the bunk.

Every time Shawn moved, Drake smelled her shampoo. It had kept him awake this long and would probably continue to keep him awake. If this was the case, he should head back out to the galley. Or bunk on JP's side of the room. Drake rolled over again and pushed his pillow into a more comfortable shape, resigned to not sleeping.

Chapter Five

"Next string, guys," Cap spoke over the loudspeaker, rousing the crew from their sprawled positions in the galley. Shawn pushed JP's feet off the end of the bench so she could slide out. She pulled the suspenders of her rain pants up, and grabbed a pair of dry gloves from the box next to the door.

Drake shoved the door open and they emerged into the cold as Shawn yanked her hat down further over her ears. The last time Shawn had looked at a clock it had been eight p.m. That was sometime during the last string and they'd been working for eighteen hours at that point. She didn't know what time it was now. She was tired, and there were only a few more pots to go. She could do this. She would do this.

JP yawned and moved to the rail as Drake reeled in the first trap. Everyone was stiff and sore, but kept pace. Shawn and Drake wrestled the pot onto the launcher and shook the crabs out.

"Look out," JP yelled.

Shawn turned as the crab pot clipped Drake in the side of the head. She cursed and rushed toward him as he fell over the railing.

"Man overboard," she screamed, dodging the dangling pot. Without thinking, she climbed onto the rail and jumped. The cold water took her breath away and she swallowed the briny liquid, gasping in shock. She had been trained for this, but it had been years since she'd done it. And then she'd worn a cold-water survival suit.

She swam hard toward where she'd last seen Drake, doing her best to ignore the thirty-five degree water. It seemed like she swam for hours, but it was less than a minute before she saw Drake, face down in the water and unmoving.

Not bothering to curse, Shawn turned him onto his back. He was unconscious but breathing. Shawn sighed in relief. She knew from her stint in the Coast Guard hypothermia would set in quickly. If they were in the water much longer, survival was unlikely.

Shawn took a deep breath, wrapped her arm around Drake's chest and swam toward the boat. JP threw a life ring past Shawn and she caught it as he pulled it back in. After wrapping the rope around Drake, she fought to tie a knot.

She could feel her legs going numb and her arms were already like lead clubs. She knew if she didn't attach herself to the rope, she'd never make it. Unable to fashion another knot, she clumsily wrapped the rope around one arm several times and tried to paddle toward the boat with the other. Her body trembled and she knew they needed to get out of the water. She saw Cap peering over the rail and felt herself being yanked through the water toward the boat.

They'd hooked the rope from the life ring onto the winch and were reeling them in like a crab pot. Relieved she'd make it back on the boat, Shawn turned her face to Drake. He hadn't moved since she'd reached him. She brought her hand to his mouth to check if he was breathing and didn't feel any breath.

She slapped him before realizing her hand was numb. When she moved her face next to his and felt shallow breaths coming from his nose and mouth, she closed her eyes in thanks that he was still alive. She felt herself being lifted and shivered at the wind on her wet skin and clothes.

When she opened her eyes she was lying on top of JP.

"You okay?" he asked.

Shawn nodded. "Drake?"

"He's unconscious but alive," JP said and stood. He

grabbed Shawn's hand and when he pulled her to her feet she shrieked at the pain in her shoulder.

JP let go and she fell back to the deck, cradling her arm against her chest. Tears rolled down her face and she bit her lip to keep from screaming again.

JP scooped her up and Shawn struggled, stating, "Drake's worse off than me. I'm fine."

"His arm isn't flopping around like that, so I guess you're in worse shape." JP kicked the door to the galley open and settled Shawn on the bench. "What's with the arm?"

"Drake?" Shawn asked through numb lips when Cap entered the galley.

"He's fine."

"Is he conscious?"

"Yeah, he said he wanted a hot shower." Cap cast a worried smile at Shawn. "He'll be fine."

"Come on," JP said. "You need to get out of those clothes."

Shawn stood propped against the wall while JP peeled off her soaked jacket and rain pants. She'd lost her boots in the sea and Cap helped her balance while JP pulled off her wet socks. When they tried to pull her sweatshirt over her head, she gasped. "I think my shoulder's dislocated."

JP turned to Cap. "Now what?"

"She still needs to get out of those clothes and into something dry. We'll deal with her arm after she's dry."

"You okay with that?" JP asked Shawn.

Shawn squeezed her eyes shut and nodded.

"It might hurt."

Shawn whispered, "Probably."

"Can you help?" JP asked.

Shawn opened her eyes, clenched her jaw and worked her uninjured arm out of her sleeve. With a grimace, she pulled it over her head, closing her eyes. After a few seconds she whispered, "Pull it off."

JP worked the sweatshirt down her arm as gently as he could but she still moaned.

"Okay?" he asked.

She bobbed her head once and pulled the blanket Cap offered tighter around her body. After a few steadying breaths, she met JP's gaze. "What's wrong with you?"

"I've never seen a dislocated shoulder. I don't know what to do for it."

Shawn was still cold, but getting out of the wet clothes was a huge improvement. "Can you get some sweats from my pack?"

JP left the galley and returned. Shawn sat down after putting on the dry clothes and pulled the blanket back up over her shoulders. "Can you help Cap put my shoulder back into place?"

"I'd rather not," JP answered.

"Too bad," Cap said as he entered the room. "It has to be done."

"I know. I'll do it but I'd rather not."

"What's the matter?" Shawn teased. "You didn't used to have a problem with people being injured."

"Yeah, I did. That was the worst day of my life." JP's face paled. "I couldn't even look at your arm without wanting to puke. Actually, I did puke while you were passed out."

Shawn looked at Cap. "We, uh, used to know each other. When we were kids."

"I figured that out." Cap handed Shawn a glass of whiskey he'd poured.

"I took some of the pain pills from the first aid kit."

"Drink it," he ordered.

Shawn drank it and said to Cap, "My grandfather was a fisherman."

Cap nodded. "I know."

"How did you know?"

"We were friends," he said. "I was wondering when you were going to tell us."

"Didn't think it mattered." Shawn laughed at the sound of her slurred words. "The whiskey's working."

JP took the bottle from Cap and swallowed a shot of whiskey.

"Keep it up and you'll be in worse shape than her,"

Cap teased JP.

"I probably already am," JP replied. "Can't we keep her drunk until we get back? Do we really have to do anything with her arm?"

"It's all right. Do it now," Shawn said. She stood and wrapped her good arm around her waist.

"What do we do?" JP asked.

"You hold my body still and Cap will work the ball back into the socket."

JP groaned and rushed from the room.

Shawn looked at Cap. "I think we should probably do it ourselves."

"Has this happened before?" Cap asked and moved to stand next to her.

Shawn took a deep breath as Cap poked at her shoulder.

"A couple times. They wanted me to have surgery on it last time, but I put it off."

"Why?" Cap asked, and lifted her arm from her side.

"Chicken, I guess." Shawn gasped as Cap pushed and pulled at her arm.

"You want to sit down?" Cap asked.

Shawn sank onto the bench next to the table. She caught her lower lip between her teeth, took a deep breath and braced herself. "Now," she said.

Her eyes widened and she fought not to black out as Cap relocated her shoulder.

When he let go, she dropped her head to the table. "Wow," she groaned.

"Okay, let's get this over with," JP said as he returned to the galley.

"Too late," Cap said.

"What do you mean?" JP looked from one to the other.

"It's done," Shawn said without lifting her head from the table. "We've still got another pot."

"Leave it," Cap said. "We're heading in."

"It's going to take ten minutes to pull it up. We can sort on our way to port."

"No." Cap shook his head. "We've got two injured crew members. The only thing we're doing is high-tailing it to a hospital."

"Don't be ridiculous. We can get the last pot. I'll run the hoist. JP can wrestle it around. It's not that hard to sort crabs with one hand." She stepped back into her rain pants and winced when she pulled the suspenders over her shoulders.

"Anyone got an extra pair of boots?" she asked.

"Not going to happen. I'm the captain. Remember? And this boat is going back to land. You're done for this trip. No more work. Take a couple more pills and go lay down."

"I'm fine," she said.

"I'm glad you're fine. And I'm glad Drake is fine, too. But you're not doing anything more on this trip. If I catch you so much as lifting a finger, there's going to be hell to pay."

* * *

Shawn sat on the bunkroom floor against the edge of her bunk, letting her head fall back to the mattress. She closed her eyes and saw, in her mind, the pot hit Drake in the head again, the blood seeping out of the cut as he fell backward over the railing. She shivered and let the memory play until she swam up to his unmoving body. Then she jerked her eyes open.

She thought he was dead when she turned him over. And right then, she'd considered swimming toward the bottom of the Bering Sea until she couldn't swim anymore. In the split second it had taken her to feel his breath and realize he was alive, she'd considered giving up everything. She'd never felt overwhelming despair like that before. Not even when she learned Ethan eloped with Addi.

She didn't understand. She barely knew him and he was the first person she'd ever struck in anger. Yesterday, he'd made her want to crawl into his arms and cry about her life. Today, the thought of him being dead had made her consider suicide. What was wrong with her? She pulled her knees up and bent forward to rest her forehead on them. She took a deep breath and let go. Her entire body shook as she cried.

Shawn barely noticed JP enter the room and settle on the floor next to her. With a gentle tug, he pulled her into his arms and whispered nonsense to her while she wept.

"I thought he was dead," she whispered after catching her breath.

"Shh, it's okay. He's fine." JP rubbed her back.

Shawn wiped a hand across her face and choked back her sobs as she scooted away from JP, not wanting to cry in front of anyone, even someone who had helped her get dressed. "I didn't know Cap knew Grandpa," she said, trying to remove the focus from her tears.

"I didn't, either," JP replied. "I didn't tell him."

"I didn't think you had. Do you suppose he's mad about it?"

"I don't know. If he didn't ask you if you were related to a fisherman, I guess you didn't lie."

"I should go talk to him."

"You should get some sleep."

"I'm fine," she said, and got to her feet. She turned to JP before she left the room. "Thanks."

"I didn't do anything."

"You're you." Shawn smiled and pushed the curtain out of her way.

* * *

Shawn climbed the stairs and stopped in the door of the wheelhouse. Cap was in his seat. Shawn heard classical music coming from a small stereo. She waited until Cap noticed her before moving into the room.

"How's the shoulder?" Cap asked.

"Sore. I need to talk to you about something."

"Pull up a stool." Cap lowered the volume on the stereo.

Shawn settled into the seat and watched Cap adjust

the boat's course. "I'm sorry I didn't tell you who I was."

"What do you mean?"

"I didn't tell you about Grandpa."

"I figured there was a reason you didn't mention it, so I didn't either."

"You knew all along?"

"Yep. I gave my word to Lars that if you ever came up here, I'd look after you. It was a surprise to learn you knew my brother Mike from the being in the Coast Guard though."

Cap tapped Shawn's hand where it rested on the arm of her chair. "I gave you a chance and I haven't regretted it. You've worked as hard as the rest of the crew so don't think I let you off easy."

Shawn could see the lights of another boat winking in the distance. "He left me *Poseidon*." She spoke softly, almost ashamed to admit she owned a fishing boat that was probably worth more than Cap's.

"It's a nice boat."

"I don't know what to do with it."

"You don't have to do anything with it."

"I need to decide whether to keep it or sell it."

"Not right now, you don't."

Shawn shifted in her seat.

"You'll know what to do when the time is right."

Shawn nodded in agreement, even though she wasn't sure she'd ever know the right decision.

"Where are your folks?"

"Minnesota." Shawn cringed, thinking of the explanation she owed them when she returned to land.

"What do they think you should do with it?"

Shawn snorted. "They think I already sold it. They don't want anything to do with it or Alaska."

"I guess they're not too happy that you're here?"

"That's the understatement of the year. Mom's pissed that I'm performing physical labor. And the fact that my wedding has been canceled."

"She likes weddings that much?"

"No. She likes him that much." Finding Cap easy to

talk to, Shawn continued. "He, the prince in my mother's fairy tale, eloped with my supposed best friend. Today," Shawn looked at the clock and corrected herself. "Actually yesterday, was supposed to be our wedding day."

Shawn glanced at Cap to gauge his reaction.

"Well, I, for one, am glad you were here, rather than there."

"He'd have been fine. As a matter of fact, I bet he's convinced the accident happened because I was on the boat."

"He's probably glad you were here."

They were both quiet for a bit and then Cap spoke. "He's not a bad kid."

"I know."

"He's had a rough time of it."

Shawn tried to convince Cap he didn't have to explain Drake to her. "I don't always agree with what he says, but I think he's a decent human being."

Cap rubbed his hand over his face and took a drink from his mug. "Parents want the best for their kids. We don't always know what it is, but that's all we want."

"He's lucky to have you."

"You're lucky to have your parents, too. It might not seem like it sometimes but they love you more than anything."

"I'm sure they do in their own way."

Cap turned to her and spoke forcefully. "Trust me. I know what I'm talking about. As a parent, there's nothing more painful than to see your child do something you're convinced is wrong for them."

Shawn closed her eyes. She knew her parents loved her, and every expectation and hope they had for her was because they believed it would bring her happiness.

"At some point though, you have to have faith in our judgment. You can't follow us around and make our decisions forever." She moved her head away from the back of the seat.

"That's true. Maybe it'd be easier if both sides tried harder to understand each other."

Shawn stood. "You're probably right."

* * *

When Shawn left the wheelhouse, she went into the galley, intent on chocolate milk. She opened the dirty, white refrigerator door and poured milk into a dented tin mug. After nudging the door shut with her foot, she opened the cupboard to grab the chocolate powder. She dumped some into her mug, opened the first aid kit and swallowed another pain pill.

She heard the clinking of metal against metal and noticed Drake in the corner of the booth, stirring a cup of tea. She finished mixing her milk and stayed next to the counter, uncomfortable with joining him at the table.

After a few seconds, Drake spoke. "Can't sleep?"

Shawn glanced at Drake, hunched over his mug. His posture made her think he felt as awkward as she did. She shook her head, then turned back to stare at the blackness outside the porthole.

"Thanks," Drake said.

Shawn responded without facing him. "Don't mention it. You'd have been upset about it, but you'd have done the same for me."

"How's the shoulder?"

With a one-shouldered shrug, Shawn dismissed his question and asked, "How's the head?" She rinsed her mug and hung it on a hook over the sink next to the others. As the boat rose on a swell, she lost her balance and slammed into the fridge with her injured shoulder.

Lightning shot down her arm, across her back and chest as she tried to straighten. With a whimper she caught her lower lip between her teeth to keep from screaming as she screwed her eyes shut.

When she opened her eyes, Drake was next to her. "All right?" he asked.

She nodded, clenched her teeth, and reached across the small galley to wrap her left hand around the edge of the sink, and pull herself away from the fridge. Upright, she held onto the counter and closed her eyes, swallowing to get the taste of bile out of her mouth. She opened her eyes and saw Drake directly in front of her, watching her with concern.

"Come sit down," he said, and led her to the table.

Shawn sank into the booth and realized his hands had been on her waist, holding her up.

"You need a doctor," Drake said.

"Probably," Shawn conceded and ran her tongue over her lips.

"Will ice help your shoulder?" Drake asked.

"Maybe."

"Be right back," Drake said, and stepped out of the galley. When he came back, he laid a cold pack on her shoulder. "Snow from the deck," he said before she asked. "It's more plentiful than ice cubes."

Shawn gasped at the cold and placed her head on the table again, grateful for the layer of fleece between the ice pack and her skin.

"I can call the Coast Guard," Drake offered.

"No. It's not serious enough for that." Shawn gazed at him. "They're busy. You're not calling them about a little bruise. Cap said we'd be back to port in the morning. I can wait."

When Drake didn't respond, Shawn said his name and waited until he met her gaze. "I've dislocated my shoulder before. It's not the end of the world."

"What do you do for a dislocated shoulder?"

"Pop it back in place and don't bump it on anything. Especially a fridge that doesn't seal. Sleep would help but when I fall asleep I roll over and wake up." She couldn't tell him every time she closed her eyes she pictured him lying face down in the water. Tears welled up in her eyes and she lowered her head to the table, hoping he hadn't noticed. "Maybe I'll sleep here."

"If you can sleep there, go for it."

Shawn pulled her legs up to cross them Indian style on the bench, turning her face and gazing at Drake in the dim light. "It was worth it," she whispered remembering she felt his breath on her face. How the entire sky seemed to be filled with rainbows and she had felt warmer instantly, knowing he was alive. She knew then that she had feelings for him she'd never felt before.

"What?" Drake asked, and moved to the other side of the booth.

Shawn thought of repeating herself and explaining that the arguments, insults, and bickering had all been worth it so she could be there to help him when he needed it. Instead of voicing her thoughts, she smiled.

* * *

Drake went to the bunkroom, grabbed the pillow from Shawn's bunk and hurried back to the galley. He watched her sleep for a few minutes until he felt the boat rock on a swell. "Shit," he cursed as Shawn slipped toward the floor. He caught her with an arm around her waist before she tipped out of the booth.

"What?" Shawn asked without opening her eyes.

"You were about to fall out of the booth," Drake said. "Scoot over. I'll sit here and then you'll have to knock me out of the booth before you'll fall out."

"No, that's okay."

"Move over," he ordered.

Shawn grumbled a protest but obeyed. Drake sat next to her and stretched his legs to the opposite bench. Within minutes, Shawn had forgone the pillow he'd set on the table, to snuggle against Drake, her face on his chest.

Drake sat with his arm around Shawn for a couple hours, dozing off and on, but mostly thinking. She deserved better than how he'd treated her. It's not like he was the only person in the world to be abandoned and deceived. At least he'd had his dad. Shawn didn't have anyone. Her best friend and fiancé had been unfaithful. And when she'd called her parents, her mother had betrayed her as well.

Drake had never worked on a boat with a woman. One of his best friends, Bjorn had married a woman fisherman, Kirima. Her father owned a fishing boat and after they were married, Bjorn joined their crew. Their first trip out, the boat had capsized. Kirima and two of the other crewmembers had survived. Her father and her new husband hadn't. Drake knew if Bjorn hadn't married Kirima, he'd have been on *The KayLeigh* and would probably still be alive today.

To top it off, his mother had telephoned him right before he'd left for the boatyard the day he'd met Shawn. He suspected from the lack of surprise Cap had shown, his father had been expecting the call. Thinking of his mother was enough to put Drake in a bad mood. Speaking to her and learning she was coming to see him was the proverbial icing on the cake. All the way to the boat, he'd cursed. When he'd arrived and saw some of the leased pots needed mending, he was enraged.

If that wasn't enough, he'd found out his father had hired a woman. Drake believed, at that moment, his life couldn't possibly be any worse. He admitted now his father was right; he wouldn't have trusted any new hand. Trust was something that had to be earned. So was respect.

Shawn had earned both from him. Very few of the hands he'd crewed with in the past had a work ethic like hers. On the entire trip, she hadn't complained about anything other than his behavior.

And she had risked her life for him. He wasn't sure he would have survived if she hadn't been there. JP was his best friend, but he wasn't a strong swimmer.

Shawn shifted in the crook of his arm and he raised his hand to touch her hair again. He worked the binders loose and dropped them on the table before unbraiding her hair and running his fingers through it. He bent his head and inhaled the scent of her hair again. It was lemony and even remembering his mother used lemon shampoo when he was little didn't prevent him from smiling.

Drake's breath caught when Shawn groaned against his throat. She pressed a kiss to his skin.

Drake jerked away.

"What?" Shawn asked and sat up, bumping her arm against the table. "Ow," she said, opening her eyes wide.

"You were talking in your sleep," Drake said.

"What did I say?" Shawn asked.

"I'm not sure. I couldn't make it out."

"Oh." Shawn scooted away from him.

"Feel any better?"

"Not as tired. It doesn't hurt so bad."

"Doesn't hurt so bad, as in you might be able to sleep?" Drake asked and stood.

"Maybe." Shawn yawned. "If I can get my mind to quit spinning in circles."

"What's on your mind?"

"Nothing important."

Drake fixed two cups of tea and sat across from her, sliding one over to her. "I keep seeing that damn pot coming at my head every time I close my eyes."

"I suppose so." She sipped her tea. "Thanks for the tea."

Drake nodded back at her. "What do you keep seeing?"

Shawn looked down at her mug and spoke so softly Drake had to bend forward to hear her. "You lying face down in the water. Not moving."

"I'm sorry."

Shawn lifted her face and Drake was surprised to see her eyes were wet. "I thought you were dead," she whispered.

Stunned at the emotion he saw, Drake looked away and tried to make light of the situation. "No such luck," he joked.

"What?" Shawn's expression changed from sad to angry.

"I was making a joke. Trying to get you to laugh."

"And you think I'd laugh if you were dead?" She rose to her feet and carried her mug to the sink, dropping it in with a clatter.

"Hang on a second." Drake rose from his seat and grabbed her uninjured arm. "Stop and listen to me." He tugged, turning her toward him, and tipped her head up. After he slid her hair back with both hands, he was shocked to see tears coursing down her face. "Oh, man." He pulled her to his chest and wrapped his arms around her. "This is what I was trying to avoid. You looked like you were going to start crying and I thought a joke would prevent it."

He nuzzled the top of her head and whispered. "But now you're crying and you're pissed at me. I can't win for losing with you, can I? I'm glad you saved my life. And I'm sorry you thought I was dead."

Shawn didn't respond. He could feel her body shaking in his arms, and it wrenched at his heart. He cradled her head to his chest and rocked back and forth on his feet. He rubbed his hand up and down her back, pausing for a second when her arm wrapped around his waist.

He slid his hand down the back of her head to rest inside the collar of her sweatshirt on her neck, tugging on her hair to get her to look up at him but instead she pressed her face harder against his chest. Her hand had slipped under the hem of his t-shirt and pressed against his skin. When her sobs ceased, he dropped his hands and shifted away, even though he didn't want to. She felt good in his arms, and he liked the pressure of her arm around his waist.

Shawn looked up at him and Drake wiped away the last of her tears. "Better?"

She stepped back, bumping into the wall, and smiled at him. "Yeah. Thanks."

Drake's mouth went dry. "No problem, it was the least I could do since I made you cry."

Shawn kissed his cheek. "I'm glad you're alive," she whispered, and left the room.

Drake stood against the counter for a few minutes, then moved back to the table. He sat down and played with the hair binders on the table. He'd never been so affected by a kiss before. It was a kiss on the cheek, like someone would give their grandma, but that didn't stop him from having feelings about it, both physical and emotional.

He looked up when JP entered the galley, and slid the binders into his pocket as JP spoke, "She needs a doctor."

Drake agreed. "Yeah, I wanted to call the Coast Guard but she wouldn't let me."

"You guys spoke?"

"A little." Drake looked down at the table, touching the cheek she'd kissed, speaking almost to himself, "She thought I was dead."

"I know."

"She cried about it."

Drake's voice was soft and JP leaned forward before repeating, "I know."

Drake looked up at his friend.

"In the bunkroom, when I went in there, she was crying," JP said.

"Really?"

"Maybe there's more to it than you know," JP suggested.

"You might be right." Drake stood. "I'm going to take over for Dad. He could probably use a nap, and it's not like I'm going to sleep."

"Why not?"

"Every time I close my eyes I see that damn pot coming at me." And he'd probably be thinking about Shawn all night, but he wasn't going to tell JP that.

"Well, if you decide to try sleeping, I can take a turn at the wheel."

Drake climbed up to the wheelhouse without acknowledging JP's offer.

Chapter Six

"Do you ever use the bunk?"

Shawn looked up at JP from the bunkroom floor. "Yeah, when I'm sleeping."

JP sat on his bunk, elbows on his knees. "What's that?"

Shawn pulled her feet toward her and looked down at the picture in her hands as if she didn't remember what it was. "Ethan," she said and handed it to him.

JP looked at the picture. Shawn was standing next to a tall, thin blonde guy who had his arm around her shoulders. They were laughing at the camera. "Your boyfriend?"

"Ex-fiancé. We were supposed to be married yesterday."

"Why weren't you?" JP handed the picture back.

"Because he got married to my best friend a few days before I came up here." She snorted with sarcastic laughter. "I guess 'ex-best friend' would be the correct term."

"Is that what you're running away from?"

"Not them, really. More like trying to get away from the pain, I guess."

"Is it working?"

"In a way, yes. In another way, no." She swiped at her eyes. "I've turned into such a cry baby lately."

"I suppose you have a valid reason. You going to tell me what's working and what isn't?"

Shawn pursed her lips. "I haven't thought about them

in a few days. Only yesterday because of the date. So, I guess that's working."

"That's good."

"The problem is that..." She looked away and fidgeted.

JP laughed when she moved her left arm so she could rub at the scar on it with her hand in the sling.

"Bit of a nervous tick?" he asked and pointed at her arm.

Shawn looked down. "Yeah, I guess so." She didn't look up before she continued. "What's not working is, for some reason I like Drake." She glanced up to see JP's reaction.

"Why does that fall into the category of not working?"

"Because I don't need a relationship right now."

"Why not?"

"Ever hear of rebound dating working out?" When he didn't respond, she continued. "I'm not getting involved with him."

JP put his hand on hers. "What went through your head when you thought he was dead?"

Shawn looked away. "I wanted to help him."

"Don't lie to me. You once told me I was your best friend and you told me all your secrets. I know the name of the first boy you kissed. Remember?"

"Of the first *man* I kissed." She could joke about it now, because her feelings for JP had changed.

"Yeah, that too." JP laughed. "You never could lie very well. Might as well 'fess up."

"I wanted to sink to the bottom and give up," Shawn whispered. "Like this world wasn't worth my time if he wasn't in it."

JP tugged on her hand until she met his gaze. "You ever feel that way about Ethan?"

She shook her head.

"You know why?"

She shook her head again.

"'Cause you didn't love him."

She pulled her hand away from him, unwilling to admit it to herself, let alone JP. "I don't love Drake, either."

"Why aren't you sleeping yet? Every time I've ever taken one of those pain pills it knocks me right out."

"I can't." Shawn yawned.

"Why not? You're obviously tired. Does your arm still hurt?"

"Not too bad."

"So?"

"If I close my eyes, I see him, face down in the water, not moving," Shawn whispered with a trembling lower lip.

"Why do you suppose that bothers you so much?"

She was quiet for a while, then met his gaze. "Probably because I love him."

"So, what are you going to do about it?"

"I told you I don't need a relationship right now."

"You're right. Right now, you need sleep."

Shawn moved from the floor to her bunk. "I'll try."

"Would you feel better if he was here?"

Shawn shot a look of fear at JP. "You can't tell him."

"Course not. I'll just go up to the wheelhouse and tell him he needs some sleep."

"I don't think it'd help."

"You're probably right." JP stood and stretched. "But he does need some sleep, too."

Shawn closed her eyes and thought about what JP had said. Being dumped by Ethan didn't bother her anymore. If he hadn't run off with Addi, Shawn wouldn't have come to Alaska. She wouldn't have met Drake. Shawn felt her lip tremble at that thought.

It hit her with full force then. JP was right. She was more upset at the prospect of never meeting Drake than she was about Ethan marrying Addi instead of her. She wasn't sure she liked this feeling, but at least now she knew it was love.

* * *

Drake left the wheelhouse, and stopped in the galley to dump his cold tea down the sink drain on his way to the bunkroom. He pushed the curtain aside so light from the hall fell on Shawn. Her back was to him and she was still. After gazing at her for a few seconds, he let the curtain fall. This was as good a place as any to stay awake. He didn't want to admit, even to himself, that he wanted to be in the same room as Shawn.

He crossed to the bunk, stripped down to his boxers, stretched, then hoisted himself up to the top bunk and slid into his sleeping bag. Staring out the porthole next to his head, he yawned. The only sleep he'd had since regaining consciousness on the boat was while he'd sat next to Shawn in the galley. And before that, they'd all worked for more than twenty hours with nothing but catnaps between the strings of pots.

Shawn's voice broke the silence. He couldn't understand what she was saying and presumed she was talking in her sleep again. He rolled to peek over the edge of his bunk and said her name softly.

Her legs kicked in her sleeping bag as she whimpered. In an instant he was beside her, gathering her close. No one was more surprised than Drake at the soothing words that whispered from him and the gentle rocking motion he'd begun.

Shawn moved closer. Her eyelids opened and as recognition passed across her face, her body tensed against his.

"Sorry I woke you," she said.

"I wasn't asleep."

"Why not?"

"Can't."

Shawn nodded to show she understood.

Drake straightened from his crouched position next to her bed, stunned when Shawn caught his hand.

"Stay," she whispered.

Drake froze, unsure of what she was asking.

"Please." She pulled on his hand again and moved over on the narrow bunk.

He lay down next to her, being careful not to bump her shoulder. "How's the shoulder?"

"Okay." She yawned.

"Yeah, me too," Drake said.

"You too, what?"

"Tired."

"So, go to sleep."

"I told you. I can't."

Shawn laughed and turned her face toward him. "Aren't we a fine pair? Neither of us seems to be able to sleep, even though it's likely we need it worse than anything."

"Yeah, you're probably right." Drake didn't see anything humorous about being terrified to close his eyes, but he could feel his mind calming as Shawn whispered to him.

"What's the first thing you're going to do when you get to land?"

"Offload the catch."

Drake felt Shawn kick him in the leg and laugh before she said, "Idiot. I meant after you're done working."

"Probably go home and get cleaned up." Drake turned his head toward Shawn.

"Then?"

"Go out for a drink with JP. You?"

"Order a big, greasy pizza and take a long, hot bath."

Drake didn't hear anything after that. He visualized Shawn in a bathtub full of bubbles. He wasn't surprised that the imaginary bathtub was the one in his home. Her head against the back, with her hair trailing down the sides of her face; the damp ends touching her shoulders and bubbles barely covering her.

"Sleeping?" Shawn asked.

Drake considered not responding, so he could continue envisioning it. "Nope. Thinking."

"About?"

He chuckled. "I'm trying to picture you eating greasy pizza."

"What do you mean?"

"Greasy pizza doesn't seem like your style."

"So what's my style?"

"I'd guess pasta, wine and classical music."

"Why do you think that?" Shawn asked.

"You seem to have the demeanor of someone who likes that kind of stuff."

"You mean hoity-toity?"

"No. I mean classy."

Shawn laughed. "Don't my parents wish?" After a moment, she continued. "You're right on the pasta, but only lasagna. I don't like wine and I hardly ever listen to classical music."

"I suppose it would make your parents happy if you were more..." Drake's voice faded away as he searched for the right word.

"More presentable?"

"No. Not presentable, I was going to say 'more like them'."

"Yeah, I bet they'd like it if I was. But I'm not. If what I am isn't good enough for someone, anyone, that's their problem. Not mine."

"Even your parents?"

After a few seconds Shawn responded. "Especially my parents. Aren't parents supposed to love and accept their children no matter what?"

"I thought so." Drake was quiet for a bit, and then turned on his side to face Shawn. He draped an arm over her and pulled her close. "You should come out with us for a drink." He wanted to see her after the crabbing season ended but was afraid to ask her out on a date.

"Maybe I will." Shawn nestled closer and yawned again.

"You don't have to stay awake to entertain me," Drake said. "I'm probably going to go read for a bit." He had no intention of leaving the bunk, but wanted her to get some sleep.

"Will you stay until I fall asleep?"

"Yeah, I'll do that."

"G'night, Drake."

"Good night, Shawn," he replied, enjoying the sound of his name in her voice. After tugging the zipper of her sleeping bag down, he rolled onto his side, dropped his leg over hers, and in a matter of seconds he was asleep, with a smile on his face.

* * *

Shawn stepped into the galley as Cap descended from the wheelhouse. After she swallowed a pain pill with a glass of water, she started to put on her gear.

Cap held up his hand to stop her. "You won't need that," Then he turned to Drake and said, "JP and I'll offload the catch. You two are going to the hospital."

"I'm fine," Shawn and Drake said at the same time.

"You're going." Cap slammed his fist on the table.

"I'll go after the catch is taken care of," Shawn said. "I'm finishing the job I started."

"You heard me. You're going to the hospital. Period." Cap spoke over his shoulder as he returned to the wheelhouse.

Shawn turned to Drake. "You gave in pretty easy."

"When he's in this mood there's no point in arguing. It's like trying to convince a polar bear to move to Florida."

"What's he upset about?"

"JP gave his notice."

Shawn bit her lower lip. "I didn't know he'd made up his mind."

"You knew?"

"He told me he was considering the possibility because he wants to spend more time with his wife and daughter. I didn't know he was serious. And if I did know, I wouldn't have thought it was my place to break the news to Cap."

Drake held up a jacket for her. She slid her uninjured arm into the sleeve and allowed Drake to button it over the sling as *The KayLeigh* bumped against the dock. He led her off the boat, down the dock, and across the highway to his beat-up pickup. The paint was peeling off in big chunks and the bottom of the body was rusted, but it ran well. He unlocked the door on the driver's side and reached across to unlock the other one.

Shawn yanked the door open, and Drake said, "Sorry for my ungentlemanly behavior. It only unlocks from the inside."

"I'm pretty sure I can open a door for myself," Shawn replied.

"Hang on." Drake swept his arm to the middle of the seat, dragging the CDs and papers away so Shawn had a place to sit.

"What? You actually listen to music?" Shawn teased. "I figured you listened to the weather station." She settled onto the seat and grabbed the door handle. She tugged and cursed.

Drake looked over at her holding her right arm in her lap, as she tried to appear nonchalant. "What's wrong?" he asked.

"I forgot," Shawn replied through clenched teeth. She reached across her body with her left hand and pulled the door shut.

"Here." Drake leaned across the truck, opened the door a few inches and slammed it.

Shawn gasped and he turned his face to look at her. There was sweat on her forehead and her bottom lip was clenched between her teeth. Her eyes were screwed shut.

"You okay?" Drake asked.

She nodded. "No hospital."

"You need to see a doctor."

"Fine, but not a hospital. I don't like hospitals."

Drake started the truck. "I think you need to go to the Emergency Room." He turned down the radio when it came on too loud.

Shawn put her hand on his. He looked toward her. "It's not an emergency. Take me to a clinic or something."

"If that's what you want."

Shawn closed her eyes, leaving her hand on his.

Drake glanced down at their hands and noticed how

smooth hers was, even though she'd been on a crab boat in the wind and water. He used his left hand to move the gearshift out of park to keep his hand under hers. He told himself he did it for her, not because he liked having her touch him.

After a couple minutes of grumbling at every unavoidable bump in the road, he glanced over at Shawn and saw her eyes were open again. "Better?" he asked.

She ignored the question and closed her eyes without looking at him. "This is one of my favorite CDs," she said after a few minutes.

Drake nodded, then realized her head was turned toward the window. "Hey."

Shawn looked at him.

"You did good out there." He turned his attention back to the road.

Shawn squeezed his hand before pulling hers away.

Drake stopped at a light and looked over at her. Her head rested on the back of the seat and faced him, with her eyes closed. He noticed her eyelashes were long and curled gently where they lay on her skin. Her complexion was pale to start with, but she was so peaked now she looked green in the early dawn light.

This could have been different if they'd met at a different time and place. Her attitude annoyed him on the boat, but he had to admit he admired it, too. She was scared of certain things, but it never stopped her. It didn't even seem to slow her down. She worked harder than lots of the hands he knew.

He pulled into the parking lot of the clinic and stopped in front of the door. He read the hours and looked at her. She needed a doctor much worse than she'd let on. She turned sideways so none of her bruises touched the seat and opened her eyes.

"Hey."

"You look bad."

"Flatterer." Shawn attempted to smile as she pulled her leg up onto the seat.

"We're here," Drake said and jerked his head toward

the clinic.

Shawn shifted to look and returned her gaze to Drake. Her eyelids were open halfway, like they'd been since the accident. Drake figured it was from the pain pills she'd been taking.

"They don't open for another half an hour. Do you want to wait or go to the emergency room?"

"Wait."

"You sure? You really look awful."

"I'm sorry I didn't get gussied up for you. I will next time, I promise." Shawn's words were slurred and the smile she aimed at him was crooked.

"How do you feel?" he asked.

"Dopey." Shawn closed her eyes.

Drake watched her from the corner of his eye while he straightened the junk on the seat of his truck. He was reaching for a CD next to her leg when she grabbed his hand and he froze.

Her eyes were open. "Sorry," she said.

"For what?" Drake glanced down at her hand, which still held his.

"Sorry you don't like me." Shawn's eyes closed.

Drake watched a tear squeeze between her eyelids and cursed himself. "Don't cry about it. I'm not worth it."

Shawn opened her eyes. "Who's crying about it?"

Drake turned on the seat and cupped her cheek in his hand. With his thumb he wiped away her tear. "You're crying about something."

"Oh." Shawn closed her eyes and pressed her face into Drake's hand.

"I'm sorry I'm such an ass." Drake's voice was rough. He pulled his hand away from her face and was surprised to hear a tiny whimper. "What's the matter?"

"Nothing," she said and took his hand in hers.

He didn't want to have any of the feelings he was having for her. He tried to extricate his hand from hers, but she wouldn't release it. He marveled at the blueness of her eyes when she opened them and how they darkened as he watched. She tugged on his hand and he relaxed his arm, allowing her to bring it back to her face. After kissing the palm of his hand, she pressed it against her cheek.

"I like the way your hands feel," she whispered.

Drake was taken aback. "What?" he said.

"You heard me."

"You're out of your mind from those pills." Drake pulled his hand away, shaking his head.

Shawn slid across the seat and whispered, "No, I'm not."

Drake froze in shock when she draped her leg over his, and touched his face before kissing his cheek. When she pulled her lips away, Drake raised his hands to hold her face still, trying to think straight while her hand traveled down the side of his neck and around to twine in the hair at the back of his head.

Shawn's eyes drifted shut as Drake's thumbs brushed over her face and he kissed her mouth. Drake felt Shawn's hand under the collar of his shirt. He released her face, skimming his hands to her waist and lifted her onto his lap before sliding to the center of the bench seat.

When their mouths parted, both were gasping for breath. Drake wrapped his arm around Shawn's waist and pulled her down on top of him. She nuzzled against his throat and inhaled deeply. "Wow."

"What was that?" Drake asked in a daze.

"I think it was a kiss."

"I've never had a kiss like that before."

"Never?"

Her eyes seemed clearer and she didn't look as pale. Drake shook his head in response to her question. "You?"

"Well, I was engaged."

Drake looked away from her, hurt she'd bring up her ex now.

"And he never kissed me like that." She kissed the side of his throat again. "He never smelled as good as you."

"You said Old Spice makes you want to puke."

Shawn inhaled. "It's not so bad when it's mixed with fish and crab slime." She licked the side of his neck. "And you."

"I should have given you some pain pills earlier." Drake joked.

"Why?"

"If this is how you react to them..."

"What?" Shawn pushed away from him.

"Just think. We could have spent the past week doing this instead of fighting."

Shawn moved further from him. "You think I'm doing this because of a pain pill?"

"I have no idea. I honestly don't know what happened."

After looking out the passenger window, Shawn faced him again. Drake recognized the same expression as when she'd punched him and he recoiled a bit, nervous he might be hit again.

Without meeting his gaze, Shawn said, "I kissed you because I wanted to. The pills may have lowered my inhibitions a little, but they didn't change my mind about you." She took a deep breath and blurted, "Getting to know you is what made the difference."

Astonished, Drake swallowed. He searched for the correct response, but couldn't find the words to express himself. If he didn't understand what he felt for her, how was he supposed to explain it? Even to the person who most deserved to understand?

"I'm not what you think I am." He grinned in what he hoped was a light-hearted, devil-may-care manner, and continued. "That kiss was great but your parents are right." As Shawn opened her mouth to speak, he corrected himself. "What they'd say about me would be right. I'm no good and we'd never amount to any more than a good time."

"That's probably the stupidest thing you've ever said." Shawn pulled the jacket around her body like a shield and Drake regretted his words. He should have said something else. Or nothing at all. He'd meant to say he wasn't looking for a relationship, instead it sounded like he wasn't interested in anything more than sex, which wasn't his style.

"Shawn," he said, and reached toward her. He had to straighten this out so she didn't think he was into one-night stands. That kiss had addled his brain though.

When Shawn met his gaze, he said, "That didn't come out right."

"Yeah," she said. "I understand."

"How can you understand when I don't?"

"Don't worry about it. I made a mistake. It's happened before and will probably happen again." With a pointed look at his hand on hers, she pulled away and glanced at the clinic, asking, "What time is it?"

Drake glanced at his watch as a woman flipped the sign to open in the clinic door.

"Don't bother." Shawn opened the truck door.

"That went well," Drake said under his breath and rushed to catch her. He reached the double doors right before her and yanked a door open.

Shawn narrowed her eyes and opened the other door to pass through.

"Is it really that hard to accept my help?" he asked, following her inside.

Shawn approached the desk in the reception area. "Can I see a doctor?" she asked.

"I'm sorry. His schedule is full. You're welcome to wait and we'll try to squeeze you in."

"Sounds good."

"Are you one of Dr. Smith's patients?"

"No, I'm not from around here."

"Okay. Fill this out and I'll get you entered into the computer." The nurse slid a clipboard and paper across the counter.

"How long do you suppose it'll be?" Drake asked the receptionist as Shawn walked away with the forms.

"I don't know," she smiled at him. "Why are you here?"

Shawn struggled out of the jacket, sat down and started writing on the form.

"Dislocated her shoulder a couple days ago." He

looked at Shawn who was paling into the range of green again. He lowered his voice. "She says she's fine, but I think she's lying."

"Why don't you take her to the hospital?"

"She refuses."

"I'll see what I can do." The receptionist stood and disappeared through a door into the exam area as Drake sat beside Shawn. Shawn glanced at him and shifted to hide her paperwork from him. "No copying."

"I'm not filling one out."

"You should. Cap said you were supposed to see the doctor too."

"I don't need one and he knows it. He only said it so you'd agree."

Shawn cursed under her breath, displeased with how the two Richards men had manipulated her into getting treated before finishing her job

* * *

After the doctor reset her shoulder and put it in a sling, Shawn walked out of the clinic with Drake.

"Do you have a place to stay?" he asked.

"I'm not picky. Anything with a shower is good for me." She pointed across the street at a cheap-looking hotel. "There's perfect." She checked for traffic and crossed the street.

"Are you sure? You can stay at the house," he offered as he followed.

"No, thanks."

Her speech was a little slurred and her witty responses were a little slower than normal from medication. They approached the desk and Shawn registered. She pulled a crumpled bill from the pocket of her jeans.

"I got it," Drake said and tossed a credit card on the counter.

"I'll pay for my own room." Shawn yawned.

"You can pay me back as soon as Dad pays you,"

Drake replied. Most people would consider Shawn's current demeanor pleasant, but Drake already missed her normal attitude. A meek Shawn was pretty dull.

"What's so funny?"

"What do you mean?"

"Why are you smiling?"

"I was thinking how much easier it is to get along with you when you're all doped up."

"Go to hell."

The clerk at the desk fumbled with Drake's credit card and Shawn yawned again. When she started to sway on her feet, Drake wrapped his arm around her waist and pulled her against his side. He signed the register, pocketed his card and the key, then nudged Shawn in the direction the clerk indicated. When she stumbled, he picked her up, and cradling her in his arms, he strode down the hall to the door of her room.

"Shawn," he whispered.

"Hmm?"

"Wake up."

"No."

"I have to set you down so I can open the door."

Shawn dropped her head against his shoulder.

Drake swallowed. It was getting harder to control his feelings for her. He was ready to pick up where they'd left off in the truck. "Shawn, I'm going to set you down. You have to stand up for a minute."

"No." She put her arm around his shoulder and nuzzled her head against him.

Drake chuckled and balanced her against his body while he unlocked the door. He kicked the door shut and set her on the bed, helping her out of her jacket and shoes.

She pulled the blanket over herself and burrowed her face into the pillow.

"I'm going to take off," Drake said.

Shawn nodded into the pillow.

"Shawn?"

"What?" she mumbled.

"Did you hear me?"

"You're going to take off, right?"

"Yeah. I'll write down directions to the bar if you're feeling up to it tonight."

"Okay."

* * *

Shawn walked out of her hotel and turned left. She stopped in front of a dark window to look at her reflection and fussed with her hair for a few seconds, wondering why she was doing this. Drake wanted someone to fool around with. At least that's how it had seemed in his truck. She told herself she wasn't going to see Drake. She had woken up and was hungry. The bar would have some sort of food.

"Liar," she said to herself. She knew she was going because she wanted to see Drake.

She stepped inside the bar and took a moment to adjust to the dim light and noise. While scanning for faces she knew, a man approached and asked her to dance. "I'm meeting someone. Thanks anyway."

Drake was standing halfway down the bar, talking to a man she didn't recognize. Shawn looked him over. She was used to seeing him in rain gear and ratty clothes, unkempt and unshaven. Her behavior in his truck made it obvious she was okay with that appearance.

She was struck by how well he cleaned up. A person would never guess he was a fisherman. He was wearing khaki pants, a white t-shirt and a leather jacket. He looked like an executive dressed down for a night out on the town with his buddies, except for his beat-up work boots.

Shawn cursed when someone lurched into her, hitting her shoulder. She jerked away and bumped into a woman who, in turn, pushed her into another patron.

"Hey, take it outside." Shawn heard a voice that sounded like Drake's but her vision was blurred from the pain. She stuck her hand out, searching for the wall to support herself.

"Shawn!"

Shawn opened her eyes with a groan to find Drake peering at her.

"Is there gel in your hair?" she asked.

"What are you talking about?"

Shawn reached up and touched his hair. "There is, isn't there?"

"Are you okay?"

"My shoulder hurts, but it's getting better. I was surprised to see you all spiffed up."

"Spiffed up?"

"Who're you trying to impress?"

"No one. These are the clothes that were clean."

Shawn glanced around and saw people watching them.

"You okay?" Drake asked again.

"I'm fine." Shawn stood.

Drake pointed across the room and said, "JP's over there."

Shawn followed Drake to the corner table and sat down when he pulled out a chair for her.

JP looked happy as he spoke. "Evening kids. Did you come together?" Shawn looked at Drake in question. She didn't understand why he knew where JP was seated but hadn't joined him.

Drake shook his head in response to JP's question. "I'll be back in a bit." He met Shawn's gaze. "Quit being stupid." He returned to the bar. Apparently, he didn't intend to join them now, either.

Shawn watched until he disappeared and then looked around the table.

"What did you do now to warrant the 'quit being stupid'?" JP asked.

"He's playing nursemaid. He should look into a career in a hospital instead of on *The KayLeigh*."

"Hi, I'm Shawn," she said with a smile to the two women seated at the table. She knew from pictures near JP's bunk the blonde was JP's wife, but had no idea who the other one was.

"Sorry, I've got rotten manners." JP dropped his arm

around the blonde's shoulders and gave her a hug. "This is Celia."

"It's great to meet you. I've heard how wonderful you are," Shawn said.

Celia pursed her lips and looked away after saying, "Hi."

Shawn shifted her gaze to the Inuit woman, who smiled and said, "I'm Kirima."

"So what did the doctor say about the shoulder?" JP turned toward Kirima. "Shawn dislocated her shoulder pulling Drake from the water a few days ago."

"Bet he's pissed about that," Kirima said, and took a sip of her drink.

Sensing Kirima was a person she could like, Shawn relaxed. When she felt JP's gaze, she looked at him. "What?"

"The doctor. The shoulder. What was said?"

"He had to reset it. It wasn't seated quite right, but he said you did a good job."

"I didn't have anything to do with it," JP replied with a look of discomfort.

"Fine. Cap did a good job," Shawn replied before her attention wandered again.

"And?"

"And what?" Shawn knew her lack of focus was the problem, but JP's continual questioning was getting on her nerves.

"What else did he say?"

"Like what?"

"Like how long are you off *The KayLeigh*?"

"It hasn't been decided yet," Shawn said.

"I asked what the doctor said. Not what's been decided?"

"I need surgery. It's been dislocated too many times. He's pretty sure it's not going to stay put."

"When's that going to be?"

"When's what going to be?" Shawn met JP's gaze. She wasn't annoyed with his questions now; she was being difficult for the fun of it. The look of exasperation on JP's face made her forget about Celia's cold greeting and at least someone was talking to her.

"The surgery. You are having the surgery. Right?"

"I don't know. I'll have to sit around doing nothing for at least six weeks."

"You could clear up that matter we talked about, regarding *Poseidon.*"

Shawn cocked her head to the side and looked at JP. "Yeah, I could. If I knew what I was going to do." Shawn didn't want to discuss her grandfather's fishing boat. She turned and looked at the crowd, searching for a glimpse of Drake.

"He won't be back."

Shawn looked at Kirima, surprised she'd been addressed by someone other than JP. "What?"

"Drake." Kirima smiled. "He won't be back while I'm here."

"Why do you say that?"

"He doesn't like to be around me."

"Why?"

Kirima swirled the ice in her drink. "Because it reminds him of the past."

Shawn looked at Kirima, trying to see her as Drake might. About the same height as Shawn, her skin was a beautiful tan shade. An emerald green blouse and black pants made her stand out from the flannel and faded denim in the bar. "You guys dated?"

Kirima looked sad. "No, he was my husband's friend. Drake never liked that we were together."

"Oh." Shawn glanced at JP and Celia as they moved to the dance floor. Watching the two of them, so obvious in their love caused a twinge of pain. She doubted she would ever appear that way with anyone. "How long have they been married?"

"They've been together since high school. Married for five or six years, I think."

After their dance, JP and Celia returned to the table with their arms still around each other. Without taking his eyes from Celia, JP said, "We're going to call it a night. Do either of you need a lift?"

Shawn declined. "No, I'll walk back to the hotel. It's only a couple blocks."

Kirima grinned at the couple. "I'm surprised you guys stuck around this long. I'll talk to you in a few days."

Shawn tried again. "It was nice to meet you, Celia."

Celia nodded. They left and Shawn kept looking around the bar.

Kirima stood. "It was nice meeting you. If you're going to stick around town for a while, I'll probably see you again."

Shawn looked up at her. "Yeah, it was nice meeting you too."

"Once I leave, Drake'll be back."

"What do you mean?"

"The way you're searching the room for him is a pretty good indication that you're interested in him."

Shawn smiled sheepishly. "I don't know why. He doesn't like me."

"Don't worry, you'll figure it, and him, out." Kirima waved her fingers and walked toward the bar.

When she disappeared into the crowd, Shawn looked back to her glass of soda. She picked up the paper coaster and methodically tore it into strips. When a waitress neared the table, Shawn ordered a burger and fries.

"You look lost."

Shawn jumped at the voice behind her and turned her head. "No. I'm waiting for a friend." The man who spoke was about the same height as Drake, muscular, and wore the standard fisherman uniform: jeans, flannel shirt and work boots.

"Who? Maybe I know them," he said.

"Drake Richards," Shawn answered and turned toward the crowd again.

"Yeah, I know Drake. Are you dating him?"

"No, we're just having a drink."

"I'm Mark Evans." He held out his hand.

"Shawn," she replied and awkwardly shook his hand with her left hand.

"Oh yeah, you're the chick that snuck onto *The KayLeigh*."

"I didn't sneak on to the boat. Cap hired me."

"I bet that pissed Drake off."

"Probably a little." She wasn't sure where the conversation was going and felt relieved when Drake approached.

"Hey," she said to him. "I just met Mark."

Drake gave an abrupt nod. "Evans," he muttered.

"Richards," Mark replied in the same tone. "How was the catch?"

"Good. Yours?"

"About the same." Mark smiled at Shawn. "When you get tired of fishing on a small boat, look me up. We'll find room for you."

Shawn lifted her arm and the sling. "Won't be for a while, but thanks for the offer."

Mark grabbed a piece of the coaster and scribbled on it, before handing the paper to her.

Shawn glanced at it and, when he walked away, Drake asked, "Did I interrupt something?"

"Not that I know of." Shawn crumpled the paper and tossed it back on the table. "He introduced himself." She sipped at her soda. "Why is it that everyone I've met tonight has said the exact same thing about you?"

"What did they say?"

"Bet that pissed Drake off."

"What?"

"That's what they said. Kirima said it when JP told her how I messed up my shoulder. Mark said it when he learned Cap hired me."

They sat at the table without speaking until the waitress returned with Shawn's meal and flirted with Drake for a few minutes. Shawn and Drake made small talk while she ate. When she finished, she stood. "Want to dance?"

Drake shook his head.

"Fine. See you around." Shawn left a twenty-dollar bill on the table, pulled her jacket on, and started toward the door. She nodded at Mark as she passed him.

"Leaving?" Mark asked.

"Yes," Shawn responded.

"Need a ride?"

"I'll walk, thanks."

"Do you mind if I walk with you?"

Shawn figured he was probably harmless, but she didn't want to be alone with him.

"I mind," Drake said and stepped between Shawn and Mark. "Sorry I took so long," he said to Shawn.

Shawn smiled at Mark. "Thanks anyway."

* * *

Once they were outside, Drake said, "Unless you'd prefer his company."

"That depends. Are you going to be pleasant?"

Drake chuckled. "How's the shoulder?"

"Better."

"Think how much better it'd be if you had the surgery done."

"I'd rather not."

"Why?"

Shawn stopped and leaned against a light pole.

Drake turned toward her. "What are you afraid of?"

When Shawn didn't respond, he met her gaze and guessed. "Not being in control?"

"I hate not being in control. That's why I seldom drink."

"Really?" Drake looked at her in disbelief.

Shawn pushed away from the pole. "Would you believe that I've never been 'falling down drunk'?"

"Seriously?"

Shawn started walking again. "Yup."

"We can go back to the bar and get you completely wasted."

"I don't think it's a good idea to mix pain pills and alcohol."

"You're probably right." Drake stopped and Shawn kept walking, so he said, "Your hotel is here."

"Yeah, I know."

"Why are you still walking then?"

"Why not? Don't you ever feel like moving for the sake of moving?"

"I figure I get enough exercise when I'm working."

"Well, thanks for seeing me back to my room. You don't have to accompany me on my walk."

"I'm not invited?"

"If you want to come with, you can. I meant that you don't have to join me. I figured walking these two blocks would put you over your exertion limit for today."

"You're funny." Drake punched her lightly in the arm.

Shawn laughed and they walked aimlessly for a few blocks, before Drake grabbed her hand and pulled her down a narrow path off the street.

"Where are we going?" Shawn asked.

"You'll see," Drake said over his shoulder. A couple minutes later, they emerged from the scrub brush on a point of rock that stuck out over the bay.

When Drake stopped and pointed up, Shawn tipped her head back. "Oh." The northern lights were clear and bright. She stood, staring up at the sky.

"It's beautiful," she finally whispered, afraid her regular voice would break the spell she felt under.

"Yeah," Drake agreed.

Shawn glanced at Drake and saw he was looking at her instead of the sky. "What?" she asked.

"I didn't say anything."

"I know. I meant what are you looking at?"

"You."

"Why?"

"Because I can."

Shawn didn't know what to say, so she turned her attention back to the sky until she felt Drake tugging on her hand.

"What?" she asked, and looked at him again.

"You never lose control?"

"Not if I can help it."

"What about earlier today?"

"You mean at the clinic when I was doped up so they could reset my shoulder?"

"No. Before that."

"I don't have any idea what you're talking about."

"In the truck."

"Oh." She could feel her face growing warm.

"Or didn't you lose control then?"

Shawn pulled on her hand, embarrassed to be discussing it. She wasn't about to tell him she'd had no idea where she was, or even who she was, when she was kissing him. She was afraid he'd reject her if he knew she wasn't interested in a casual relationship.

Drake held onto her hand and stepped toward her. "Maybe we should relive the experience so you can tell me if you were in control."

Shawn yanked her hand away. "This is stupid."

"What's so stupid about it?" he asked, and shifted closer to her.

"What's the point you're trying to make?" She turned and strode toward the street.

Drake grabbed her hand and pulled until she faced him. Then his mouth was on hers.

Shawn held still, unwilling to react as he wanted her to. When he cupped her face and pulled away far enough to focus on her eyes, her resolve crumbled.

"I wasn't trying to make a point. I wanted to kiss you again." He was so quiet, Shawn wasn't sure whether she'd imagined it.

He kissed her again. "I hoped you were in the same frame of mind."

Shawn felt herself weakening as he ran his fingers over her face. When his thumb danced across her lower lip, she sighed.

He nuzzled the side of her face and whispered, "I'm pretty sure I wasn't in control."

Shawn wrapped her good arm around his neck and kissed him fiercely.

When they pulled apart, he asked, "So?"

"So, what?"

"Are you in control?"

Shawn laughed and nodded.

"Really?"

"Yeah, and so are you."

"How do you figure?"

"Well, we must be, because otherwise at least one of us would be missing some clothing."

Drake's raised eyebrows revealed his surprise at her response. "Really?"

"Yeah."

Drake turned toward the hotel. "Let's go somewhere where that can happen."

"It's not."

"What do you mean?"

"I'm not going to sleep with you, Drake."

"I have no intention of sleeping." He bent his head and started whispering in her ear but she interrupted.

"That's not going to happen."

"Why not? We're both adults and we both want it. Why shouldn't it happen?"

"I don't sleep around."

"I never thought you did." He kissed her again.

"Don't." Shawn pulled away. "I'm not going to have sex with you. It has to mean something to me."

"It will."

Shawn broke away and jogged toward the hotel. When she reached for the door, Drake was right behind her. For not being a runner, he had kept pace pretty easily and wasn't even out of breath, which made Shawn wonder about his stamina in other endeavors. She forced her mind away from that thought when he spoke.

"Do you want to continue this conversation inside or out here?" he asked.

"Not at all," she replied.

"That's not an option." He followed her inside and down the hall to her room. "I want you."

"It's good to want things. But you shouldn't expect to get everything you want in life."

Shawn unlocked her door and stepped inside. She swung the door shut and Drake stopped it from closing with his foot.

"What's the problem? It's obvious you want me too," he asked.

Shawn didn't know how to explain she was scared that a physical relationship would cause her to want more from him. She wasn't eager to fall further in love with him, knowing it would never amount to a serious relationship.

"Can I come in?"

"No." Shawn wanted him, but only if it meant as much to him as it did to her.

"Fine. I'll stay in the hall."

Shawn's expression told him she didn't believe him.

"I'm pretty sure if I kissed you right now, you'd be all over me."

Shawn knew he was right, but wouldn't admit it.

"Care to try it and find out?" Drake asked.

Shawn panicked and backed away as he stepped toward her.

"Is he bothering you, miss?" A fat, bald man in a sweat-stained tank top asked from across the hall as he emerged with an empty container on his way to the ice machine.

"No, we're just talking."

"Yeah, I'm trying to figure out why she doesn't want to sleep with me. She sure seemed to earlier when her hand was in my pants."

"Oh for chrissake. Get in here before you say anything else." Shawn yanked Drake into the room, slamming the door. "What the hell are you thinking?"

"I had no idea that you cared so much what people think of you."

"I had no idea you could be so stupid."

"Why's it matter what some guy you'll never see again thinks you did or didn't do?"

"My hand wasn't down your pants."

"I know." Drake grinned. "But I got what I wanted by saying it."

"No." Shawn shook her head. "You didn't. I'm not having sex with you."

"You're sexy but that doesn't mean all I want is to crawl into bed with you."

"Yeah, right." Shawn dropped her jacket on the chair next to the door and kicked off her shoes. She walked to the other side of the room and turned to face Drake who remained by the door.

"Nervous?" Drake asked.

"No. What would I be nervous about?"

"Me being here?"

"Don't be ridiculous. I was stuck on a boat with you for how long?"

"Yeah, and while you were stuck on that boat with me, I noticed you rub that scar when you're worried about something."

Shawn looked down. He was right; she was tracing the scar on her arm with the middle finger of her other hand.

"What's with the scar?"

"I told you. I broke my arm."

"How'd you break it?"

"I was messing around with a friend and fell. Not a big deal."

"Must have fallen pretty hard to break two bones."

"There was this guy that I liked when I was fifteen. I was trying to impress him. He climbed up a tree, so I followed him. I freaked out when it was time to climb back down and fell. Not a big deal." Shawn changed the story a little so he wouldn't know she'd been on *Poseidon* when she fell.

"And the scar reminds you that you took a chance and it turned out bad?"

Shawn jerked her head up to look at him. "Yeah, I guess so."

"So, every time you do something you don't think you should be doing, you rub at it?"

"I don't know. Never really thought about it."

"I see." Drake moved her jacket from the chair and

sat down. "Did it ever cross your mind that I might enjoy your company and not want to leave yet?"

"Why would I think that?"

"I don't know. Because it's the truth?"

Shawn remained silent.

"I'll leave," Drake said after a few minutes and stood.

Shawn saw him glance at her scarred arm and forced her hand to be still. "You don't have to go." She enjoyed his company but didn't know what to say or do. And knowing he enjoyed being around her made her question her decision not to sleep with him.

"Nah, I think I'll call it a night."

Shawn said his name as he reached for the door handle.

When he turned, she said, "I'm not going to sleep with you just to sleep with you. I'm not like that."

"Yeah, we already covered that."

"You don't understand."

"I probably understand better than you realize."

"Fine, tell me what you understand and I'll tell you how close you are."

"You don't trust me. There's nothing else to be said about it."

"You don't get it."

"No, you don't get it." Drake frowned. "It's not any easier for me to trust someone than it is for you. At least I'm willing to take a chance."

"But..."

"No. There are no buts about it. You either jump or crawl back down to the ground."

"What's that supposed to mean?"

He opened the door. "Did you ever stop to think about how you broke your arm?"

"Yeah. I told you. I did something I knew I shouldn't do."

"No. You took a chance and tried something different. But you didn't break your arm until you tried to return to what you knew. It's all in how you look at it." He stepped into the hall and pulled the door shut behind him.

"Drake, wait..." Shawn rushed to the door. When she opened it and looked down the hall, he was gone.

She closed the door and watched out the window. Not seeing him anywhere after a few minutes, she sank down on the bed, switched on the television, and didn't fall asleep for hours.

Chapter Seven

Shawn woke the next morning and after dressing, she tested her arm's range of motion. When the pain wasn't severe, she dropped the sling on the bed and left the room.

It was four in the morning and as she rounded the corner from the hotel, she saw another runner headed toward her.

Shawn smiled when she recognized Kirima. "Hi," she said and stopped.

Kirima halted, too. "Morning. What happened to the sling?"

"It's in the hotel. Kind of hard to run with your arm strapped down."

"You're a runner, huh?"

"Yeah. And it's a great morning for a run," Shawn said.

"I was heading out, but if you're interested we could get a cup of coffee instead."

"I'm not a coffee drinker. If you don't mind I'll tag along with you on your run."

Kirima agreed and the two jogged away from the hotel. After a few minutes, Kirima said, "Did he come back after I left you at the bar last night?"

Shawn nodded, knowing Kirima was asking about Drake. "So did some guy named Mark Evans."

Kirima's step faltered. "Really?"

"Yeah, I think he offered me a job on a boat."

Kirima laughed and sped up. "If you want it, you got it."

"Why do you say that?" Shawn adjusted her pace to match Kirima's.

"No reason. What happened with Drake?"

"He walked me back to the hotel."

"And?"

Shawn sped up a little. Kirima matched her pace.

Shawn laughed. "We fought. It's what we do."

"Drake has that effect on a lot of people."

They ran in silence for a bit, then Kirima said, "How far do you normally run?"

"About four miles."

Kirima grinned. "Getting tired?"

Shawn laughed at her. "Not really. You?"

Kirima took off in a sprint. "Last one back to the hotel has to buy breakfast."

Shawn raced after her. "I don't know where I am," she gasped when she pulled abreast of Kirima.

"Take a left on the next street. Then it's about four blocks."

Shawn kept pace with Kirima until she recognized her surroundings. "I'm completely broke," she gasped and concentrated on beating her opponent.

She was running as fast as she could, struggling to breathe, when someone stepped out of the hotel onto the sidewalk. She cursed and tried to stop.

Kirima stepped off the sidewalk into the street and Shawn recognized Drake as she plowed into him.

"What the heck?" Drake twisted so he landed between Shawn and the sidewalk.

Shawn raised herself off him. "Sorry."

"Are you okay?" he asked.

"Yeah. It's fine." Shawn turned to Kirima. "I think it was a tie."

"Nah, you won." Kirima waved. "I'm going to head home for a shower. I'll meet you over there in an hour." She jerked her head at the cafe next to the hotel.

"What are you doing?" Drake asked. "And where's your sling?"

"It's inside," Shawn said. "And I went for a run."

"Obviously."

"What's that mean?" Shawn tipped her head at him quizzically.

"It's pretty apparent that you went for a run."

"So, why'd you ask?" Shawn turned away without waiting for an answer. "Were you here for a reason?"

"Yeah, I was going to ask you if you wanted some breakfast." Drake followed her to her room.

"Sure, you can join Kirima and me." She opened her door.

"No. That's quite all right."

"Why don't you like Kirima?" Shawn removed her shoes and went into the bathroom.

"I'm going to leave," Drake said, as Shawn turned on the shower.

"Why?"

"You're clearly busy."

"Not really," Shawn said when she walked out of the bathroom to retrieve clothes from her pack. A glance in the mirror revealed Drake, slumped in the chair, legs stretched out and crossed at the ankles. His elbow was on the arm of the chair and his chin was propped on his fist. The look on his face intrigued her and she wondered what his gray eyes were seeing as they stared at the floor.

She turned toward him. "What's up?"

"Nothing. I remembered that you were broke and I wanted to make sure you got some breakfast. Dad'll get your pay to you sometime today."

Shawn stretched side to side at the waist. "That's cool. But what's bothering you?"

"What makes you think something is bothering me?"

"You look as jittery as I normally am. Did you run out of soothing herbal tea?" Shawn walked into the bathroom, partially shutting the door behind her.

"I'm going over to the boat. I'll see if Dad has your check ready yet."

Drake's voice moved toward the door and Shawn decided it was as good a time as any to tell him the truth about her feelings. She took a deep breath, then said,

"Before you leave, I want to tell you something."

"What's that?"

"You're right," Shawn said.

"What? I thought I heard you say I was right. That can't be what you said."

"Funny." Shawn spoke as she shampooed her hair. "I said you're right. I'm chicken and I don't take chances. I'm not interested in a one-night stand." She tipped her head back and let the hot water stream over her hair, knowing she wouldn't be able to hear his reply if he made one. "But I am interested in you." She spoke softly, unsure whether she wanted him to hear that admission.

She heard the door close. Telling him hadn't been the end of the world, even though he didn't feel the same way. She finished her shower and turned off the water as she wiped at her tears. He wasn't worth crying over if he was only interested in sex.

She dried off and put on her bra and underwear. She yanked her jeans on and walked out of the bathroom, combing her hair. She froze when she saw Drake sitting in the chair. "I didn't know you were still here," she said.

"It looks better already." He gestured at her shoulder.

Shawn glanced down at her shoulder. "It feels a lot better today."

"Good."

Shawn dropped the comb and pulled on a shirt, not knowing what to say. She didn't know if he'd heard her confession and wasn't sure how to broach the subject. She didn't even know if she wanted to bring it up.

"Will you go out with me tonight?" Drake asked, as he looked at the floor.

"Sure," she said, and sat on the bed to pull on socks and shoes. She glanced at the clock as she put on her coat and stood. "Kirima is probably waiting for me. Are you sure you don't want to join us?"

Drake rose from the chair. "No, thanks."

Shawn reached for the door and he caught her hand and said, "I'm not positive, but I don't think I'm interested in a one-night stand, either."

Shawn searched his face for a sign he was lying. When she didn't find any, she smiled.

Drake caressed Shawn's cheek and kissed her after saying, "Besides, I'm pretty sure one night wouldn't be enough for either of us."

He stepped away, and said, "I'll pick you up at seven?"

Shawn agreed, and the two of them walked out of the room together.

* * *

Shawn entered the nearly empty diner, spotted Kirima and slid into a booth across from her. "Sorry I'm late."

"Fighting again?" Kirima grinned.

"A little. He's taking me out tonight."

"Is 'fighting' a euphemism for something else?"

Shawn shook her head and smiled, before scanning the menu and ordering pancakes. "No, it's not."

"Are you staying in Kodiak for a while? Planning on returning to wherever you came from? Going back out on *The KayLeigh*?" Kirima sipped her coffee.

"I can't fish right now. I suppose it'll be a couple weeks before the doctor will give me the okay. And I don't have any reason to return to where I came from, so I might as well stick around. Why?"

"Going to live in the hotel?"

"Nope. I have a place lined up, but I need some advice." Shawn had an appointment with her grandfather's attorney later in the day. Once she received the keys, she intended to move into her grandparents' house north of Kodiak.

"What kind of things do you need advice on?"

"A couple things. First and foremost, Drake Richards."

"He was Bjorn's friend. Not mine."

"Don't you know anything about him?"

"I've known him most of my life and he tolerated my presence until Bjorn died. He's never said it, but I gather from his behavior he thinks I caused Bjorn's death in some roundabout way. Other than that, I don't know anything. JP could tell you whatever you want to know, I'd guess."

Shawn was disappointed Kirima didn't have any information to share. "Fine. Next topic. Fishing."

"I know a little about fishing," Kirima answered.

Shawn liked Kirima even more for her understated ways. JP had told her Kirima owned *The Norseman*, one of the largest fishing boats docked in Kodiak.

"How do you go about captaining a boat with a crew of men? And how do you tell the guy you're interested in that you own a fishing boat?"

"Why? Do you intend to buy and captain a fishing boat? And I suppose it would depend on the guy."

Shawn took a long swallow of her milk and faced Kirima. "My last name's Nilsen."

"Is that supposed to mean something to me?"

"Ever hear of *Poseidon*?"

Kirima's eyes widened. "That Nilsen, huh?"

Shawn nodded. "And in case you were wondering who the guy is that I'm interested in, that would be Drake Richards."

"Yeah. I knew that already. So, what's the real question?"

"I inherited all of my grandfather's stuff. That includes *Poseidon*."

"Why's that a problem?"

"I'm pretty sure Drake will consider it a problem. Especially since I never bothered to tell him."

"Why not?"

"I didn't think it was important."

"Don't tell him."

"He'll find out."

"Yeah, he'll find out. But if you don't think it matters, it doesn't matter."

"You think I should try to build a relationship without telling him who I am?"

"Are you keeping the boat? Are you going to stay here forever? Do you think he's your soul mate?"

"I don't know. I only know I've never felt the way I do when he's around."

"Does that matter?"

"I really don't know." Shawn finished her pancakes and slid the plate to the edge of the table.

"Why do you think you need to decide all of this before you go out with him?"

"Not so much before I go out with him. Definitely before we end up in bed together, and I've got a feeling that's going to happen pretty quickly."

"That's the feeling you haven't felt before?"

Shawn laughed. "Yeah, even with my fiancé, I didn't feel like that."

"Fiancé? That might change my advice." Kirima raised her eyebrows.

"Ex-fiancé, sorry. The 'ex' part is new and I keep forgetting to include it. He eloped with my ex-best friend and my savings account."

"Oh. Then my advice involves plotting his and her death."

"It was meant to happen. If it hadn't I wouldn't be here now."

"So, you're one of those people who believe everything happens for a reason, huh?"

"Sometimes. Other times I'm convinced the world is out to screw me."

"I feel that way most of the time." Kirima changed the subject. "What are you wearing on your date?"

"Probably what I'm wearing now."

"You can't wear jeans and a sweatshirt out on a date."

"He doesn't care what I wear. He's seen me covered with cod slime when I haven't showered in days."

"Yeah, but you weren't on a date with him." Kirima glanced at her watch. "I have to get to the dock. Meet me at five tonight." She scribbled an address on a napkin and left it on the table when she stood.

Shawn rose as well. "Thanks for breakfast. Next time's my treat."

* * *

Drake knocked on the door of Shawn's room and slid his hands into his pockets. Even after remembering her teasing the night before about being all spiffed up, he'd taken care with his appearance again. He was wearing a pair of dark blue jeans, a gray button down shirt and a black leather jacket. The previous evening he hadn't wanted to be obvious about it, but tonight, for their date, he'd changed his shirt three times, trying to find just the right balance between looking careful and careless about his appearance.

Nervous, he pulled his keys from his pocket and tossed them from hand to hand as he waited. After a minute he knocked again, wondering if Shawn had changed her mind about their date.

"Hang on a minute," Shawn called.

"Whew," Drake said as he stuffed the keys back in his pocket. She hadn't changed her mind. He chuckled to himself. *It's not a blind date, man. You know her and you like her. It's even pretty certain she likes you. Otherwise she'd never have agreed.* Drake shook his head. No woman had ever affected him like this before.

"Sorry," Shawn said as she opened the door.

Drake froze, speechless as he looked at her. She'd poured herself into a strapless red dress and heels so high they made Drake wonder how she could walk in them.

"What? Is something wrong?" Shawn asked.

"No." After swallowing and clearing his throat, Drake continued. "You look great."

Shawn twirled, causing the dress to flare out around her legs. "A little different than what I wore on the boat, huh?" she asked.

Drake repeated, "You look great."

"So do you." Shawn pulled a long black jacket from the coat hook behind the door. "Is it too much?"

"Too much? What do you mean?"

"Too dressy? What did you have planned?"

"I don't remember." He reached up and ran a lock of

her hair through his fingers. She'd left it loose and it brushed her collarbone. With a tentative glance at her face, Drake skimmed his fingers over the discoloration on her shoulder. When she gasped, he jerked his hand away. "Sorry."

"For what?"

"I didn't mean to hurt you."

"You didn't." Shawn held the coat toward him.

"Oh, yeah." Drake helped her into the jacket, cursing himself for forgetting his manners.

They left the room and, as they exited the hotel, Shawn spoke. "Kirima said I couldn't wear jeans and a sweatshirt."

"Sure you could. But this is a good look for you." He offered her his arm. "Let's see if we can find something worthy of your appearance in this town."

Shawn laughed. "We don't have to go anywhere fancy. We can have burgers."

"There are a couple of decent restaurants in town. And I happen to have reservations at one of them."

* * *

"Would you like to dance?"

Shawn looked up from her fidgeting hands. Cautious of being close to him, she considered declining, but the attraction she felt for him overpowered her anxiety. "I wouldn't have guessed you were the dancing type. Especially after you refused last night."

"Not normally. But I was hoping for a chance to show you off."

"If we went out on the dance floor, everyone would feel sorry for you. I can barely walk in these shoes."

Drake glanced under the table at her shoes. "You never wore those on the boat."

"No kidding." Shawn giggled at his teasing. "They're Kirima's. The dress is, too. I certainly didn't bring them with me."

Drake pressed his lips together and gave a quick nod.

Curious why Drake responded in such a way to the mere mention of Kirima, she asked, "What did I say to make you look so unpleasant?" Doubtful he'd tell her, she still thought she'd try.

Drake curled his lips into a smile Shawn suspected wasn't genuine and reached across the table to take her hand and pull her to her feet. "Come on. I promise it'll be easy. All you have to do is follow my lead."

"You mean let you be in control?" she teased.

His eyes gleamed with humor. "Yeah. Think you can do it?"

Shawn relaxed, happy he didn't seem to be dwelling on thoughts of Kirima, and put her other hand on his shoulder.

They started to move to the music, and Drake said, "You do too know how to dance."

"Of course. My parents thought it was important. It's not something I do often, though."

Drake pulled her closer. "Me neither, but I figured it was my best shot at feeling you against me tonight."

"What kind of line is that?" Shawn murmured, and slid her hand up his shoulder to touch the back of his neck.

"It's not a line if it's true." He dipped his head and kissed her. When he pulled away, she rested her cheek on his shoulder.

"What is it about you?" she whispered.

"What do you mean?"

Shawn considered not answering, but keeping her feelings to herself hadn't been successful up to this point in her life. She might as well be honest. "There's something about you that makes me want things I don't remember ever wanting before."

She forced herself to continue even though she was terrified of baring her soul. "Like being taken care of and having someone who worries about me. Someone who treats me like a princess." She lifted her gaze to meet his. "Even as a little girl I never wanted to be a princess. I'm perfectly capable of taking care of myself and have never wanted anyone to do anything for me."

Drake smiled and Shawn forged ahead, encouraged.

"But something about you makes me want all these things that are out of character. It's like I don't know myself, anymore."

"I assume it's my sparkling personality," he joked, and guided Shawn to the table. "Our food is waiting."

They talked about childhood mishaps while they ate, then returned to the dance floor. This time, Shawn nestled against Drake like she belonged there. She didn't let herself think about the future; she just enjoyed being in his arms.

"Shawn," Drake murmured, causing her to lift her gaze to his face without moving her head from his shoulder.

"Hmm?" She didn't want the feeling to end.

"It's not just you," Drake whispered as he smoothed her hair from her face. "I feel things I've never felt before, too."

Shawn felt a surge of something course through her. Unsure whether it was hope for a possible future with Drake or love for him, she whispered, "You were wrong."

"About what?" His hands skimmed over her shoulders and arms.

"Dancing wasn't the only chance you had to feel me against you." She drew him off the dance floor. "Take me home with you," she urged.

Chapter Eight

The next morning, Shawn woke in Drake's arms. She stretched before kissing him on the jaw, then rubbed her cheek against his, savoring the feel of his beard stubble.

He smiled and kissed her. "Be right back," he said, and pulled on a pair of jeans before leaving the room.

Shawn looked around the room. There wasn't anything exciting about the room, but it was special because it was Drake's. The walls were white and a set of cheap mini-blinds covered the one window. The king-sized bed was covered with gray sheets and a blue comforter. There was a clock on the dresser next to the window and a basket of folded laundry on the floor.

Shawn rose and grabbed a t-shirt from the basket. She pulled it on and ventured from the bedroom, in search of the bathroom. She froze when she spotted an older woman coming up the stairs. "Uh," Shawn stammered.

"Hello," the woman said. "I'm Drake's mother, Patricia."

"Um, hi. I'm Shawn. I was looking for the bathroom."

"Right there." His mother pointed.

"Thanks," Shawn stepped into the bathroom and closed the door. What a way to make an impression. Wearing nothing but her son's shirt and not even knowing where the bathroom is. When she was done, she peeked around the door, hoping to avoid his mother, and rushed back into the bedroom.

Drake was lying on the bed with a black mug on his

stomach. "Hey," he said.

"I met your mother."

"Oh, yeah. She's been staying here." He pointed at a glass on the dresser. "Chocolate milk for you. Unless you prefer tea." He held up the mug.

"No, thanks. Can I borrow a pair of sweat pants or something?" She didn't want to walk back to her hotel wearing the red dress. Everyone would know how she'd spent last night if she was still wearing clothes that were obviously from a date.

"Sure, if you can't find anything in the basket, there should be some in the closet."

Shawn didn't say anything as she riffled through the basket and pulled on a pair of gray sweatpants. Thankful they had a drawstring, she tied it tight around her waist.

"What's wrong?" Drake asked, after laughing at her in his clothes.

"Your mother's going to think I'm a tramp."

"Why would she think that?"

"Well, for one, I wasn't wearing anything except your shirt."

Drake laughed. "Did she ask if you were wearing anything else?"

Shawn rolled her eyes. "And I didn't know where the bathroom was. She's going to think I followed you home from the bar."

"No, she's not." Drake stood, pulled a sweatshirt over his head and picked up his mug, before leading Shawn from the bedroom. "Let's get some breakfast."

"Actually, I think I'll just go," Shawn said when they stepped into the kitchen.

Drake's mother looked up from the stove. "Why? Did he threaten to cook?"

"I'm Shawn." She chuckled nervously, realizing she'd already introduced herself. "I'll talk to you later," she said to Drake, and reached for her coat.

"Please stay. I'm making French toast," Patricia said. "I want to get to know Drake's friends."

Shawn glanced at Drake.

"It's up to you," he said.

She'd ignore her discomfort and do this for Drake. If there was any future for them, she'd have to learn to get along with his mother. "Is there anything I can help with?" she offered.

"I've got everything under control. Unless you want to get the dishes out."

Shawn swallowed and looked at Drake, embarrassed again because she didn't know where anything was.

He directed her toward a chair. "I'll do it. Sit down."

Shawn sat at the table, and Drake set a plate of food in front of her.

The three of them ate in silence until Patricia said, "How did you guys meet?"

"Cap gave me a job," Shawn said.

"A job? Doing what?"

"Fishing, Mom. What else would she do?"

Shawn looked at Drake in surprise. "Sometimes I wonder if Cap didn't hire me just to irritate you."

"You're pretty good at that." Drake laughed. "Shawn punched me when she met me."

"What? Why would you punch him?" Patricia glanced at Shawn, and turned back to Drake. "Why did she punch you?"

"Probably because I deserved it."

"No, I'm sure that's not it," Patricia replied.

Shawn looked on in horror, convinced Patricia was going to hate her forever now because she'd punched Drake.

Drake laughed. "See? She doesn't think you're a tramp. She thinks you're a bully."

"Drake!" Shawn screeched.

Patricia looked at Shawn. "Why would I think you were a tramp?"

"Because I was in bed with your son."

"So? He's an adult. If he wants to sleep with a tramp, it's none of my business."

"Mom!" Drake snapped.

"I didn't say she was a tramp. I said if you wanted to

sleep with a tramp it was none of my business."

Shawn stood. "Thanks for breakfast." She grabbed her coat and rushed out of the house.

Drake followed her. "Shawn, wait."

"It's all right. I figured that's what would happen."

"Come on; let me give you a ride home."

Shawn laughed. "Drake, I'm perfectly capable of walking. I'm sorry your mother and I didn't hit it off, but it's not the end of the world. I've been called worse by people who meant more to me."

He kissed her before saying, "I have to do some stuff on the boat today. Come down and keep me company."

"Maybe later." Shawn turned and walked away. She didn't know how long it would take to get settled into her grandfather's house.

Drake grinned at the sight of her walking down the street in high-heeled shoes and sweatpants that were way too big for her. He went back in the house and was putting on his boots when his mother handed him a travel mug of tea. With an angry expression he took it and set it on the floor next to him. "Thanks," he said, upset his mother had insulted Shawn.

"I'm sorry. I didn't mean it the way it sounded."

"I don't care what you meant." Drake grabbed the mug, a pair of gloves, and slammed out the door.

* * *

Drake was in his truck ready to start it when he realized his keys weren't stuck in the ignition like normal. He cursed and got out of the truck, to return to the house.

"Keys?" he asked when he went back inside.

"What?" Patricia asked, looking up from the dishes she was washing in the sink.

"You took my truck somewhere this morning, I assume."

"Oh. Yeah, sorry about that. You were asleep and I had to run to the grocery store. I didn't think you'd mind."

"That's fine." Drake leaned against the doorframe. "I

don't care. I just want the keys back."

"Right." Patricia shook the soapsuds from her hands and stood at the sink, looking around the kitchen. "I think they're in my coat pocket."

"Okay. I can get them. Where's your coat?"

"I'm not sure." She glanced around again and as she started to dry her hands on her jeans, Drake grabbed the towel from the refrigerator door and held it out to her. He'd noticed in the past two days she often couldn't find things right in front of her.

"Thanks. Now where did I put my coat?"

This is how everything was with his mother. She wasn't a bad person; he'd realized that since she'd returned. She was just absent-minded. She couldn't remember where she'd left her coat less than an hour ago, so why did he think she'd remember anything about her son when she hadn't bothered visiting him in the past twenty-five years. He watched her walk into the living room where she became distracted by the news on the television.

"Mom."

When she didn't respond, he tried using her name, "Patricia." He wasn't surprised that she didn't react to someone who called her "Mom", but he was surprised how easy it had been for him to call her "Mom".

"Yes. What is it, Drake?"

"I need to get to work."

"What's the rush? Your boss isn't going to fire you."

"He won't fire me, but the engine has an oil leak. We need to get it fixed so we can get back on the water and make some money."

"Oh. Why did Shawn leave?"

"Because you called her a tramp. Remember?"

"No, I didn't. You both misunderstood me."

"All right. Do you know where my keys are?"

"Why would I know where your keys are?"

Drake groaned in frustration and ran his hand through his hair. At this point, he had to admit he'd been better off growing up without her around. She probably did mean well, but she had the attention span of a flea. He was beginning to wonder if she even realized she'd left a husband and a son in Alaska when she disappeared with Kay Leigh. It was possible she'd forgotten that detail.

Drake wiped his wet boots on the rag rug and decided it would be quicker if he went up to his room and grabbed his spare set of keys from the dresser, rather than trying to keep Patricia focused long enough for her to find her jacket. Besides, the keys probably weren't even in her pocket. The last time they'd had a discussion like this, he hadn't located the keys until he got a mug out of the cabinet for his tea.

He took the stairs two at a time and strode down the hall to the room he'd had his entire life. Today was the first time he remembered smiling when he walked into it. It was just a room, a place to sleep and store his clothing. At least it was until last night. Now it held the light, lemony fragrance of Shawn and the memory of waking up next to her. He stood inside the doorway for a moment, inhaling the aroma and considered lying back down on the bed to see if it was as comfortable now as it had been an hour ago when he woke with her in his arms.

With a shake of his head to clear the thoughts, he grabbed the spare keys off the top of his dresser, marveling, yet relieved, that Patricia hadn't lost those yet. He rushed down the stairs and called out "Never mind, I have my other keys," as he hurried out the door and got in his truck. The sooner he got to the boat, the sooner he'd finish what he needed to finish for the day. And the sooner he'd be able to see Shawn again.

* * *

He drove to the dock, boarded *The KayLeigh*, and threw his jacket on the bench in the galley where Cap was doing paperwork.

"What's the problem today?" Cap asked from the table.

"That damn wife of yours."

Cap folded the newspaper and set it aside. "You know, that's the same excuse you've used for everything that's gone wrong in the past twenty-five years. Maybe you should try a different one for a while."

Drake dumped the tea out of his mug into the sink. "And she doesn't know how to make tea."

Cap laughed. "Now you're nit-picking."

"I ran into Shawn last night."

"Oh? Is that what's got a burr under your saddle?"

"No. Your wife called her a tramp this morning."

Cap straightened up. "Are you sure? Your mother isn't always the most responsible person but she's not outright mean."

"She's a bitch and, if you weren't making me, she sure as hell wouldn't be staying at my house."

Cap corrected him. "My house. You're only living there"

"Whatever."

Cap stood, clapped a hand on Drake's shoulder. "It'll work itself out."

"I doubt it."

They walked out of the galley and descended into the engine room. "So did you and Shawn kiss and make up?" Cap asked.

"How else would Patricia have had a chance to say anything to her?" Drake smiled as he recalled the night they'd spent together.

"I don't know. I just never know with you."

They worked silently, side-by-side on the engine for the rest of the morning, each lost in their own thoughts.

* * *

When Drake walked back on the boat after lunch, he heard voices in the galley.

He stepped in as Cap said, "Good for you, girl. It's not going to be an easy row to hoe, but you've got my help any time you need it."

"Help with what?" Drake asked.

Shawn spun to face him with a look of panic on her face.

"What's going on?" Drake asked again.

"Now's as good a time as any." Cap stood. "I'm going for a walk."

Shawn stood, too, and faced Drake squarely.

"So, what's he going to help you with?"

She took a deep breath and let it out. "I'm going to keep my grandfather's boat."

"Keep your grandfather's boat? What kind of boat?"

Shawn looked away. "A fishing boat."

"That'll be nice. You can tool around in the bay."

"No. You don't understand."

"What don't I understand?"

"It's not a recreational fishing boat. It's *Poseidon*."

"What? You lost me somewhere. I thought you said that you own *Poseidon*."

"You're not lost so far," Shawn said.

"So." Drake held up his hand to prevent her from speaking so he could think. After a few seconds, he said, "Your grandfather was Lars Nilsen?"

Shawn nodded.

"You came up here and suckered my dad into hiring you because you were broke, yet you own the second largest commercial fishing boat in the harbor."

"I was broke. All I have is his property. I don't have any money."

"Property?" Drake asked and before she could reply he said, "The house."

"Two houses," Shawn said softly.

"Get out." Drake pointed at the door. "Get off this boat right now."

"Drake, let me explain."

He shook his head angrily. "You've lied to me this entire time. You lied to my father and JP. You've lied to everyone."

Shawn reached for his hand.

He twisted away from her and punched the refrigerator door. "I should have known."

"Should have known what?"

"That you were a liar."

"How can you say that? I'm still me. Everything I told you is the truth; I just didn't tell you who my grandfather was."

Drake turned to face her again. "Get out and don't come back," he said through clenched teeth.

Shawn's face fell. "Please, don't do this."

"I didn't do it. You did."

"I'm not leaving until we straighten this out," Shawn said forcefully.

Drake clenched his fists and stepped forward. He stopped directly in front of her, lifted his hand toward her face and gently brushed her cheek with the back of his hand. The panic disappeared from her expression, and he said quietly, "There's nothing to straighten out. What I thought we had turns out to be yet another lie." He dropped his hand and stepped around her.

He stopped in the door of the galley and glanced back at her. She'd turned to watch him. "I don't want to see you again." His voice was soft and dead calm as he walked off the boat. He moved to the end of the dock and waited until he saw her leave *The KayLeigh*. He glanced up and saw he was next to *Poseidon*. "Damn boat," he growled. "Damn woman."

* * *

Drake went down to the engine room, picked up a wrench and tinkered with the engine. He had enjoyed the time he'd spent with Shawn, but he was insulted she hadn't told him she owned a fishing boat. He had to wonder what else she was hiding from him.

Does it matter that Shawn owns a fishing boat? Why is it such a big deal? He tried to clear the thoughts from his head. He didn't need to think about it right now. He needed to get the engine fixed so they could get back on the water and earn some money.

He heard footsteps over his head and glanced up at

the ceiling of the engine room, wondering who it was. The footsteps moved again and a voice called out, "Hello?"

Drake didn't recognize the voice, so he didn't respond. He wasn't in the mood to deal with anyone. He wasn't paying attention and the wrench slipped, cracking his knuckles against the engine block. He cursed and threw the wrench across the room.

Within seconds, he heard the voice call out again, "Hello? I'm looking for my daughter. I heard she was on this boat."

Drake froze. "No way." He stood, wiped his hands on his jeans, and climbed out of the engine room.

"Who're you looking for?" he asked.

"Hello," a man in a leather trench coat held out his hand. "I'm Bill Nilsen. I'm looking for my daughter, Shawn."

Drake shook the man's hand and hid a smile when he saw he'd smeared grease on it. "Sorry."

"No problem," Bill looked down at his hand and pulled a handkerchief out of his pocket. He wiped at the grease.

Drake motioned over his shoulder. "There's soap in the galley."

"No, thank you. I'm fine." He met Drake's gaze. "My daughter, Shawn? Is she here?"

"Nope." After the way Shawn's mother had responded to the news about Ethan, Drake didn't feel any need to be welcoming to either of her parents.

"Has she been here?"

"Yeah."

"Do you have any idea where I might find her?"

"Didn't she tell you where she was staying when you told her you were coming up?"

"She didn't know we were coming."

"We?"

Bill pointed at a woman standing on the dock. "My wife, Deb. We wanted to surprise Shawn."

Drake looked at the woman. She was wearing white pants, high heels and a long fur jacket. "Is that real fur?"

he called over to her.

"No, it's faux."

"Good. My friend would be pissed if he thought it was real." Drake pointed at the sea lion sitting on the dock.

Deb saw Simba and stepped backward. "Oh, my God," she shrieked.

"Careful," Drake called. "If you catch one of those heels, you're going to fall in. And the water's damn cold this time of year." He grabbed a chunk of fish from a bucket and tossed it toward the sea lion. "Go away, Simba."

The sea lion gulped the fish down and disappeared into the water.

Drake turned back to Bill. "Don't you think you should have told her you were coming up here?"

"I don't think it's any of your business." Bill looked around. "Besides, she would have left town if she knew we were coming."

"Yeah, so would I." Drake turned away. "If I see her, I'll tell her you stopped in."

"Do you have any idea when she might be back?"

Drake laughed. "Has anyone ever been able to predict Shawn's comings and goings?"

Bill glowered. "You seem to know her well. Please tell her we're at the hotel."

Drake nodded, surprised to hear Bill and Deb were staying at the same hotel Shawn was at. If she hadn't spent the night at his house, they probably would have run into one another by now. He looked at Bill expectantly, and when Bill didn't speak again, Drake asked, "Anything else?" as he stepped onto the dock. "I have to run to the parts store."

He gave Bill a fraction of a second before turned and strode down the dock to his truck.

* * *

Drake parked behind the hotel and went in the service door to knock on Shawn's door, hoping to avoid her dad in case he'd returned directly to the hotel. When there wasn't any response he went to the front desk. Happy to see JP's younger sister, Bella, was working today, he asked if she had any idea where Shawn might be or if she knew what time she'd left.

"Yeah, JP picked her up a little while ago. He said they were going to take Preston to the playground after her nap."

"When does Preston nap?"

Bella glanced at her watch. "She should be up in about ten or fifteen minutes."

"Thanks," Drake said and patted Bella's shoulder.

He drove to JP's house, surprised how protective he felt toward Shawn after knowing her for such a short time. It was crazy to feel a need to protect her from her own parents, but he thought she at least deserved a warning that they were in town.

"Is Shawn here?" he asked when JP answered his door.

JP nodded. "What's going on?"

"Her parents are in town."

"What? What did you say about my parents?" Shawn asked as she came out of the kitchen.

"They're looking for you. Showed up at the boat."

"What did you tell them?"

"That I'd let you know they were staying at the hotel if you stopped by."

"Why?"

"Why what?"

"Why didn't you tell them where I was staying?"

He raised his eyebrows. "I don't like them."

"So?"

"Why should I tell them where you are? They're only going to hurt you."

"It doesn't matter. I'll go find them." She grabbed her jacket from the coat hook and pulled it on.

"I'll give you a ride," Drake offered.

"Thanks for letting me know, but no, thanks on the ride."

"You're coming back for supper. Right, Shawn?" JP asked.

"I don't know."

"Bring your parents with you." Celia suggested.

"I don't think so." Shawn pulled the door shut behind her as she left the house.

"Beer?" JP asked, as Drake watched Shawn walk down the sidewalk away from them, feeling helpless because she'd rejected his offer of a ride.

Drake looked at JP. "Sure."

JP went into the kitchen and, when he came out, he handed a bottle to Drake. "Game's on."

Drake followed JP to the living room and sank into the couch. After a few minutes of watching the hockey game, he said, "I think I messed up."

"Probably."

"I seem to have a knack for it, don't I?"

"Seems that way at times."

They were quiet for a bit longer.

"I hear your mom's back in town." JP muted the commercial on the television.

Drake snorted in disgust. "Yeah, and she's sticking around, according to Dad."

JP looked at Drake in surprise. "Really?"

"Dad suggested I might want to find another place to live."

"What are you going to do?"

Drake scratched his ear. "No clue."

"What'd Shawn's dad say?" JP changed the subject, suspecting Drake had shared all he was going to share about his mother.

"He wanted to know where she was. Said if she knew they were coming, she'd have left town. I told him I would have, too."

"Why? What's he like?"

"A pansy. He was wearing patent leather shoes. Seemed upset that I got grease on his hand. Her mom was wearing a fur jacket and freaked out when she saw Simba. I'm surprised she didn't fall in the water."

They turned their attention back to the television until Celia stuck her head in. "Staying for supper, Drake?"

"Sure, if you don't mind."

"Kirima'll be here."

"I'll behave," he said softly.

"I doubt that." Celia raised an eyebrow in apparent disbelief and returned to the kitchen.

"It's not like I have anywhere else to go," Drake said under his breath.

"There's always *The KayLeigh*," JP teased.

"I might be staying there."

"Don't be stupid," Celia said, walking back into the room. "We've got a guest room."

"No, thanks. The boat is fine."

There was a knock at the door and Kirima walked in. "JP, you have to go over to my house."

"Why?" JP asked, standing up.

Kirima glared at Drake. "You'll figure it out when you get there."

"What's going on?" Drake asked, and stood. "Is it Shawn?"

"Come on, Kirima, spill it," Celia said.

"Shawn talked to her parents."

"And?" JP said. "Why do I have to go over to your house?"

"Because I can't get her to calm down."

"What happened?" Drake asked, starting for the door.

"Ethan was with her parents."

JP spun toward Drake. "You didn't tell her that?"

"I didn't know. He wasn't with them when they were at the boat. If he was, I'd have knocked him in the water." He stormed out of the house.

JP followed him onto the porch and saw Drake had headed across the backyard through the snow toward Kirima's house. He turned to the women. "Should I let him handle it? Or is he going to make it worse?"

"I don't think you're going to be able to stop him," Celia said, and back inside, with Kirima following her.

Chapter Nine

Shawn looked up when Drake walked into Kirima's house. She'd sat down to remove her shoes at the door and hadn't moved since. She spoke through her tears. "Please don't say anything. I can't handle it right now."

Drake sank to the floor next to her. "Okay, I won't say anything." He wrapped his arms around her and pulled her onto his lap.

Shawn held herself rigid and fought to stop sobbing.

Drake gently pushed her head against his shoulder. "Go ahead and cry."

Shawn caught her breath. "They brought Ethan with them. They'd have been here sooner but they wanted to hear Ethan's side of it."

Drake kissed the top of her head while he rocked back and forth. "I didn't know he was with them. I would have told you if I'd known."

Shawn shoved her hair out of her face. She didn't think Drake's presence was helping anything. It made her want to cry about him, too. She tried to pull away, but he held her tight.

"Why are you here?" she asked.

"Because I love you," he whispered into her hair. "I can't stand to know you're hurting. I want to make it all better and I don't know how."

"It doesn't work that way," she mumbled against his chest and felt the tears start again.

"Well, if I can't fix it, I want to knock his ass into the harbor."

"Whose?"

"Ethan's. He's the one making you cry, isn't he?"

"No. It's the fact they couldn't support me, they had to hear his side of it. They're supposed to take my side, damn it! I'm their daughter."

Drake rubbed his hand up and down her spine. "You're right." He smiled against her hair. "Would it make you feel better to know your mom freaked out when she saw Simba?"

Shawn chuckled.

"So what are you going to do?" Drake asked, pleased that she wasn't crying anymore.

"About what?"

"About your parents, Ethan, your boat, me?"

"What can I do? If they really want him to be part of the family that badly, they can have him. They'll always disapprove of my choices, but I don't have to listen to it."

"That's true."

"And as for the rest, I thought I had it all figured out, but I guess not. I'll probably sell the boat."

"And do what?"

"I don't know. Maybe I'll go to Maine or even upstate New York. Get a new start, see what happens."

Shawn felt Drake tense. "No reason to stay, huh?" he asked.

Shawn sat there for another minute, knowing she'd never feel his arms again and wanting to savor every second of it. She inhaled his scent, determined to commit it to memory. She felt a lump growing in her throat and pushed away from him. She met his gaze and tried to smile as tears rolled down her face. "Thanks," she whispered and got to her feet.

"Are you saying 'goodbye'?" Drake asked, holding onto her hand.

Shawn tried to force a laugh. "No, I'm saying 'happy trails'." She tugged at her hand.

"You can't leave."

Shawn pulled at her hand again. "I can't stay."

Drake wrapped his fingers through hers. "I won't let

you leave."

Shawn closed her eyes and took a deep breath. She wanted to believe he was asking her to stay, but suspected it was wishful thinking on her part. She let the breath out and looked at him. "You don't get a say in it."

"Don't go. Please don't go." Drake ran his other hand over his face. "It'll kill me if you go."

"Don't be ridiculous. You'll forget about me in no time." Shawn's lower lip trembled and she bit it. She couldn't cry while she was saying goodbye.

"Stay with me. Marry me. Have my kids. Captain your boat. Captain *The KayLeigh*. You can burn everything I own, but don't leave me."

Shawn brought her hand to her mouth to stifle a sob. "Don't." She swallowed and tried again. "Don't say something you don't mean."

"I've never meant anything more in my life." Drake stood and took Shawn's hands in his. "I want to spend my life with you. How could I not want to marry the only woman who had the balls to punch me?"

Shawn laughed, then asked nervously, "Are you serious?"

"I'm no good at finding the right words and I don't have anything to offer you. I don't have a ring or a house or even a boat, but I love you and I want—" Drake's voice cracked and he cleared his throat. "Please marry me, Shawn."

Shawn watched in surprise as his eyes filled with tears.

"Please," he repeated and lowered himself to one knee.

"Oh my God," Shawn gasped. "Oh my God," she repeated and pulled him to his feet. "Yes," she whispered, wrapping her arms around his neck. "Yes, I'll marry you."

Drake relaxed in relief. "Thank God," he whispered and lifted her off her feet. He kissed her, set her on her feet, and said, "Should we go tell them?"

"Tell who?"

"JP? Kirima? Celia? Your parents?"

Shawn's smile faded. "No. Not my parents."

"Why not?"

"They won't approve and I'm not going to let them spoil it for me."

"You'll have to tell them sometime."

"Why?"

"They're your parents."

"So?"

Drake pulled away. "So, the only family we're going to invite to the wedding is my dad?"

"Well, your mother is still in town."

"And she will be for a while," Drake said. "They're getting back together."

"That's great," Shawn said. "Maybe you and your mom can get to know each other."

"What about you?"

Shawn chuckled. "Well, I'm pretty sure she'll think you're marrying me because I'm pregnant. But nine months from now, she'll have to accept it was for a different reason."

Drake laughed. "Let's elope."

"I'm completely okay with that. Want to drive to Vegas?"

"No, we have to get married here. With our friends."

"I know the perfect place."

"Where's that?"

"Where we met. Where I punched you." She grinned.

"*The KayLeigh*?"

"Yeah. Why not?"

"If you want to get married on a boat, why not your boat?"

"I didn't meet you on my boat." Shawn kissed him. "It's settled. Let's go tell Cap."

"I think we'll have to explain ourselves to the trio over there first." Drake jerked his head in the direction of JP's house.

"Yeah, you're probably right. And since you seem to think I must tell my parents, I'll invite them for supper tomorrow."

"What about Ethan?"

"Sure, he can come over, too. And you can thank him. If he hadn't fallen for Addi, I wouldn't be here."

"I'm still going to knock him on his ass, then I'll thank him."

"No, you won't. If anyone knocks him on his ass, it's going to be me. I've earned it."

"True." Drake wrapped his arm around her and together they walked back to JP and Celia's house.

Right before they stepped onto JP's porch, Shawn stopped. "I have one more thing to tell you."

"What's that?" Drake asked nonchalantly.

"It's about my arm."

"The scar?" Drake asked, taking her hands in his.

"Yeah, the scar."

"Shoot."

"I wasn't climbing a tree after a guy. I was climbing around on *Poseidon*." She took a deep breath. "When I was fifteen, I ran away from home. I'd never met my grandparents, but knew they lived in Alaska. When I got to Dutch Harbor, I asked around and showed up down at the dock as Grandpa was getting ready to leave port. I told him my parents knew where I was, so he let me go with him." She paused to look at Drake.

When he nodded, she continued. "We were out in the middle of the sea fishing. It was a beautiful summer day and we weren't catching anything. There was some kind of trouble with the engine, so Grandpa and his deck boss were belowdecks trying to fix it. The deckhand was in his early twenties and we were messing around. Just having fun. He climbed up on the railing of the wheelhouse and jumped into the water.

"I had a crush on him and followed him up the ladder." She smiled at Drake. "You were wrong, I wasn't afraid to jump. I just didn't jump far enough. My arm hit the rail on my way down." She rubbed at the scar. "They said I was pretty lucky."

"Yeah, I guess so. Why didn't you tell me?"

"Because of *Poseidon*."

"Okay. Why are you telling me now?"

"I wanted you to know the truth."

"And now I do." He took her hand and pulled her toward the door.

Shawn tugged him back to her. "There's more. I don't know if it matters or not, but I want to get it all out."

"What else?"

"You know the guy that was fishing with my grandpa."

"Okay. Who is it?"

Shawn's voice was so quiet he could barely hear her say, "JP."

Drake laughed. "You came to Alaska to find JP after ten years?"

"No. I had forgotten all about him until I saw him feeding Simba the first day. I didn't recognize him. I didn't make the connection. He remembered me.

"He's just a friend." Shawn looked at Drake with pleading eyes. "Please understand."

"Why do you look so worried?"

"Because I love you and don't know how you're going to react."

"I'm done reacting to it." He pulled Shawn into a hug and whispered in her ear, "I had a crush on Celia for a long time in high school. Nothing happened."

"You're not mad?"

He kissed her. "Why would I be? JP's married to Celia and you're going to be married to me. Isn't that what counts?"

"No. What counts is I love you and you love me."

"That, too." Drake kissed her again, and they went inside to share their news.

Chapter Ten

Shawn pulled a roasting pan from the oven and set it on the stovetop. She'd spent all afternoon cleaning her grandfather's house and cooking. JP had sent over a cake he had baked to show his moral support. Drake was upstairs, and all that remained was for Shawn's family to arrive.

Drake came down the stairs into the kitchen and stood behind Shawn. He wrapped his arms around her waist and kissed the side of her neck. "Want to go upstairs?" he whispered as he teased the side of her neck with his lips.

She leaned against him. "Very much. But someone said I had to tell my parents about our upcoming nuptials."

Drake dragged his hand from Shawn's waist as the doorbell rang.

"Hang on a minute," Shawn yelled on her way to the door.

Drake grabbed her arm and pulled her back. He kissed her until she was gasping for breath. When he released her, he whispered, "I love you."

Shawn went to the door, twisted the knob and pulled.

Drake laughed, unlocked the door, and opened it with his arm around Shawn's waist. "Come on in," he said.

Bill looked pointedly at Drake. "What's he doing here?"

Drake felt Shawn take a deep breath before she said, "I invited him."

Drake held out his hand. "Drake Richards. A pleasure

to meet you, I'm sure."

Bill shook his hand. "Bill Nilsen." He nodded toward his wife. "My wife Deb, and Ethan, a good friend of the family."

Drake shook Deb's hand and Ethan's without moving his arm from Shawn's waist.

Shawn forced a smile. "Come in. I'm sure you're anxious to see the place." She glanced at Drake. "I'm going to check supper."

Drake turned back to the guests. "Would anyone care for a drink? I brought some wine. There's probably beer in the fridge."

"I'll take a glass of wine, please." Deb's voice was unpleasant. She didn't sound happy to be there.

Ethan nodded. "Wine sounds great."

"Mr. Nilsen?" Drake asked.

"Sure." Bill stood in front of the mantel, looking at the family pictures Shawn had dusted and polished that morning. Deb moved to stand next to him.

Drake went into the kitchen. "See how much fun this is going to be?" He smiled at Shawn and opened the wine.

"Why are you dressed up for them?" Shawn asked under her breath.

"What do you mean?"

"Khakis and a polo shirt? You don't dress like that."

"Obviously I do, at times, otherwise I wouldn't have it to wear."

"The khakis, yes. The polo shirt? Don't be stupid. I saw the tag on the dresser."

"You would have preferred jeans covered with fish slime and a grease-stained, ripped sweatshirt?"

"It made me fall in love with you. If it's not good enough for them, that's their problem." She kissed him, and whispered, "Although my all-time favorite is you buck-naked in bed, with me."

"Mine, too," he said, and finished pouring the wine. He handed her two of the glasses and gestured toward the other room.

Shawn went into the living room and handed the

wine to her parents. Drake handed a glass to Ethan and said, "So what do you think of Alaska?"

Ethan took a sip of the wine. "Not much."

Deb turned from the fireplace. "Ethan recently returned from Aruba."

"Really? How exciting." Drake feigned interest. "What was in Aruba?"

"I was on my honeymoon," Ethan said quietly.

"What?" Drake looked around the room. "I thought you were engaged to Shawn."

Shawn spoke. "Drake, don't. It's not worth it."

Ethan moved to stand near Shawn. "I'm sorry. It shouldn't have happened the way it did."

"You're right. You should have told me you were in love with her. And you shouldn't have wiped out my savings account."

Bill stepped forward and cleared his throat before speaking. "What's the big deal, Shawn? It's not like you need the money. I'm sure the old man left you plenty."

Shawn swallowed before answering. "The big deal is he lied to me and stole the money I earned and saved. I couldn't pay my tuition, so I had to drop all my classes." She looked from her parents to Ethan, then to Drake. When Drake met her gaze, her shoulders and jaw relaxed. "You're right. It's not a big deal. Consider the money my wedding gift to you and Addi."

"You can't give us fifteen thousand dollars as a wedding gift," Ethan said.

Drake dropped his empty glass on the floor. "Fifteen thousand dollars?" he asked.

"We'll pay it back," Ethan said with an embarrassed look at Drake.

"I don't want it." Shawn glanced at the clock. "I think dinner is ready. I'll be back in a minute."

Drake followed her into the kitchen, carrying the pieces of the broken glass. "He took fifteen thousand dollars?"

"It's a small price to pay to meet you."

"I'm going to kill him."

"It's not worth it. It's only money."

"The point is he stole it from you."

Shawn turned from the counter and handed Drake a platter of roast beef. "Stop it. We're going to have supper and tell them the good news. They'll flip out and probably leave, never to speak to me again."

Drake laughed. "Let's not get our hopes up too high."

Shawn followed him into the dining room. "It's ready; come eat." She guided Drake to the head of the table and sat next to him. She knew her father was upset about Drake being seated in the position of respect, but he didn't say anything as he sat at the foot of the table.

Ethan sat next to Bill. Deb chose the chair between Ethan and Drake, leaving Shawn alone on her side of the table.

Shawn passed the platter and bowls around the table and asked Ethan about Addi.

"She's busy with school. She wants to know if you're keeping the apartment. She's moved in with me."

"No, and I don't care what she does with my belongings. She can send them to me, or she can donate them to Goodwill. I don't care."

Deb looked up from her plate. "What do you mean she can send them to you? Where will you be?"

"I'm staying here."

"Don't be ridiculous. It's time for you to grow up. Quit playing games with that Neanderthal and come back to civilization."

"Excuse me?" Shawn asked.

"You heard me. We get the picture. You picked the most vile man you could to annoy me. It's downright disgusting. But you've made your point."

"I'm not trying to make a point, Mother. And I think you owe Drake an apology."

Deb sniffed and stood. "Bill, I'm ready to leave. Ethan?"

Both men rose and followed Deb toward the door.

"Stop right there," Shawn ordered. "I cannot believe

you." She pointed at Ethan. "He stole fifteen thousand dollars from me and eloped with my best friend."

Deb looked at Shawn. "What's your point, dear? There's no need to be melodramatic."

"Melodramatic?" Shawn laughed humorlessly. "I told you he eloped with Addi and you didn't care enough about me to offer any comfort. You waited until he returned from Aruba so you could hear his side before you bothered to see if I was alive. You asked if he married her because I was sleeping around."

Drake growled at the revelation of what had been said during the phone call he overheard.

"You come up here and insult the man I love because he's a fisherman. A fisherman, not Satan. How can you say he's vile? He loves me. He's not going to elope with my best friend. He's not going to steal from me. The only reason you're in this house is because he invited you. He thought I should tell you I'm marrying him. He wanted me to give you the benefit of the doubt."

She snarled at her father. "How can you condemn him? He's a better person than Ethan is. A lot better. Hell, he's a better person than you are. You make me sick."

"You're marrying him?" Ethan asked.

Shawn was surprised anyone caught that statement in her tirade. "Yeah, I'm marrying him. As soon as I possibly can."

"You're making a mistake," Bill said angrily. "I bet he's only in it for the boat."

"Not a chance. I have my own boat. What Shawn does with *Poseidon* is completely her decision." Drake's voice was calm.

"Is that the problem, Dad? Are you mad because I inherited all of Grandpa's stuff? You refused to speak to him. You didn't even tell him about me. If you're upset about the ramifications of your decision, that's your own problem. I'm sick and tired of not being good enough for you."

She yanked the door open. "The truth is you're not good enough for me, so get out. Of my house and my life."

They shuffled out of the house toward their rental car, and she yelled after them. "Even better, get out of this state."

Drake wrapped his arms around Shawn and drew her back into the house. He nudged the door shut with his foot and bent his forehead to Shawn's. "That was fun, wasn't it?"

"Not exactly. But it's about what I expected." She pulled away and looked him in the eyes. "I didn't know you had your own boat."

"I've been trying to work out a deal on a boat up the coast a bit. It all came together today."

"Oh. So, you're not interested in captaining *Poseidon*?"

"You can captain her."

"I don't know anything about captaining and besides, I don't want to be on a boat if you're not on it with me."

"I know how you feel." He kissed her nose. "Don't worry. We'll figure it out."

Chapter Eleven

Drake and Shawn stepped onto *The KayLeigh* and went into the galley.

"Anyone home?" Drake called. He saw the coffee pot was half full and said, "He's around somewhere and won't be gone long."

"How do you figure?"

"Coffee's still hot and his cup is on the table." Drake winked and kissed her. "We could go home and go back to bed."

Shawn laughed. "When did you get so lazy, wanting to sleep all day?"

"I wouldn't be sleeping." He slid his hand under her hair at the back of her neck and held her head still to kiss her.

Shawn wrapped her arms around his waist, slid her hands under his shirt, and raked her fingertips down his spine.

Drake pulled away from Shawn and glanced over her shoulder when he heard a noise.

"Morning, kids," Cap said. "Coffee?"

"No, thanks," Shawn said making a face.

"What are you up to today?" Cap asked, and moved to the table.

Drake and Shawn followed him, noticing Patricia for the first time. Shawn's step faltered and Drake pulled her alongside him, into the booth.

"Nothing much," Drake said. "Shawn's parents showed up yesterday."

Cap looked at Shawn. "How'd that go?"

"About as expected," Shawn responded.

"How's that?" Patricia asked.

Drake squeezed Shawn's hand and answered, "Well, her mother didn't call me a tramp, but close enough."

Patricia reached out and set her hand on top of theirs. "I didn't call you a tramp, dear. At least I never meant to. I was being realistic and stating I have no right to judge Drake or what he does. I love him more than anything, but he's made it perfectly clear my opinion doesn't count."

Shawn pulled her hand away from both of them and dropped it into her lap. She didn't know if she liked or loathed Patricia. She seemed so motherly, but her way with words was a bit off-putting. Shawn still wasn't sure whether or not she was being called a tramp.

"I don't think you're a tramp for sleeping with my son. I don't know anything about you. Or him, really." Patricia smiled at Drake. "I'm sorry if you thought I was insulting either of you."

Drake turned his attention to Cap, "I need a couple favors from you."

"What's that?"

"Well, I was wondering if you could run me to Dutch Harbor in a few days. I finally got all the wrinkles worked out on that deal."

"Deal?" Patricia asked.

"I bought a fishing boat."

"Oh." She looked at Shawn. "I don't know anything about fishing."

Shawn said nothing.

"What's the other one?" Cap asked.

"Actually, there's a couple more I guess. We were wondering if we could use *The KayLeigh*."

"For what?"

Drake dropped his arm around Shawn's shoulders. He pulled her against his side and said, "For our wedding."

"About damn time."

"What do you mean 'about damn time'?" Shawn asked.

"You two have been bouncing off one another since you met. I've never seen two more pig-headed people in my life. I knew it would happen."

"How'd you know it?" Drake asked.

"She got under your skin instantly." Cap turned to Patricia. "I hired Shawn and when she met Drake he gave her a hard time about women not belonging on boats. So she punched him. Would have knocked most men on their ass, she hit him so hard."

Shawn was embarrassed at her behavior, and knew the topic would come up for the rest of their lives whenever someone asked how they met.

"Drake told me but never said how or why," Patricia said and leaned against Cap, who placed an arm around her shoulders.

Shawn closed her eyes, trying to come up with a non-offensive response.

"It's pretty simple. She made a fist and swung it at my stupid head." Drake rubbed Shawn's shoulder.

"He deserved it. I was tempted to knock him down myself," Cap added.

Drake saw the look on his mother's face and knew she wasn't going to forget Shawn had hit him. "If it makes you like her any better, Mom, she also saved my life."

"You would have been fine," Shawn said.

Cap snorted and got up to refill his coffee cup. "No, he wouldn't have. Neither of us are strong swimmers." He sat down next to Patricia. "He got knocked out and off the boat. Shawn saved him. She messed up her shoulder pretty bad in the process."

Shawn rotated her arm. "It's fine."

"What was the other favor you were going to ask?" Cap turned the subject away from Shawn's rescue of Drake.

"Well, Shawn's keeping *Poseidon*. And she'll want a decent captain for it. Can you think of anyone?"

"I'll keep my ears open."

Patricia reached toward Shawn. "When's the wedding?"

"A few days?" Shawn asked Drake. "I don't know what the laws are in Alaska."

"If you want, you can get married right now. I'm a captain of a fishing boat, you don't get any closer to God than that," Cap teased as he sat back down.

"Really? You can marry us?" Shawn asked.

"You're not getting married today." Patricia fussed. "You need guests and gifts and flowers and a dress."

"I just need Drake."

Drake kissed her. "No, we need your friends here. Without them this wouldn't have happened."

"Our friends," Shawn corrected him.

"Can I help with anything?" Patricia asked tentatively.

Shawn met her gaze. "I think I'd like that."

Patricia backhanded Cap in the chest.

"What?" he asked in an annoyed tone.

"Get out of my way so I can hug my future daughter-in-law."

Cap stood and pulled Shawn to her feet. He wrapped her in his arms and said, "Thank you and welcome to the family."

"Thanks for giving me the chance."

Patricia pulled Shawn away from Cap and hugged her gently. "I don't know much about being a mother, but I'll do my best."

Shawn sniffled. "Well, it should be interesting then. According to my family, I don't know much about being a daughter."

"Oh, don't cry, dear. We'll figure it out."

Shawn stepped back to Drake's side. "Tuesday?" she asked.

"If you want to get married Tuesday, we'll get married Tuesday."

Patricia clapped her hands together gleefully. "All right, we're going to have a busy couple days then." She grabbed a paper and pen and sat down to make a list. "Flowers, guests, cake, dress, the deck needs to be cleaned, food, attendants."

Shawn looked up at Drake. "Maybe not Tuesday?"

"No. Definitely Tuesday. You guys take my truck, go find Celia and Kirima to help you shop, and I'll take care of the guests and cleaning the deck of the boat."

"Are you sure?"

Drake nodded.

"Where do I buy a dress in this town?" Shawn asked.

"How would I know? I did like the red one you wore when we went dancing. If you don't find anything, that'll be fine."

* * *

Drake walked up to the reception desk at the hotel and asked for the Nilsens' room. Luckily, Bella was working again, so he easily convinced her to give him the information by lying and saying he was working with his future in-laws on a wedding gift for Shawn. He proceeded down the hall and knocked.

"Yes?" Bill opened the door.

"Can I talk to you and your wife for a minute?" Drake asked.

"I don't think we have time." Bill checked his watch. "We're getting ready to leave."

"So you're not even going to ask when the wedding is? Do you intend to be there?"

"I believe my daughter made it perfectly clear we weren't welcome."

Drake snorted. "Did you ever stop to think she acts that way so she can pretend it was her idea and not that you don't care enough to show up?"

"No, I'm pretty sure she doesn't want us around."

"Why?"

"Whenever we are around she treats us the way she did last night. I don't even know why we bother trying."

"You call that trying?" Drake shook his head in disbelief. "Seriously?"

Bill looked at his watch again. "Please make your point."

"You know what? You're really not worth the bother.

I came here to try and convince you to support her decision, but you're never going to do that. Are you?"

"She's an adult. She can make whatever decision she wants." Bill started to close the door.

Drake stuck his boot between the door and the jamb. "Why can't you accept her choices?"

"We've given her everything and she runs away to Alaska, again. Without bothering to let us know where she is. If she ends up alone, without a family, it's the decision she's made."

"You're upset because she came to Alaska? Or you're upset because you didn't know? Or is it because you're not going to have your perfect son-in-law?

"Let me tell you something. He's not perfect. He's a liar and he doesn't love her. Why would you think someone who doesn't love your daughter is so great?"

"Are you finished?"

"No. You made excuses for his stealing her money. You said she didn't need it. Knowing Shawn, she worked hard for that money. She's your flesh and blood. You're supposed to take her side, not that pansy-assed thief's."

"There's no need to bring Ethan into it."

"No need? He's the reason I met her. You know what she did the day she was supposed to get married? She saved my life. She didn't even like me and she saved my life. What did you do? You knew he stole money from her and ditched her at the last minute, and you didn't bother trying to comfort her? You waited until he returned from Aruba—from his honeymoon that was paid for with Shawn's money—so you could hear his side of the story. What kind of father are you?"

Drake stopped for a breath, then continued. "All because you don't like the choices she's made?"

Bill held up his hand. "No. Because she threw everything we ever gave her back in our faces. She could have gone to the finest schools. Instead she joined the Coast Guard. She refused to come home afterwards and decided to go to Seattle. We bought her a brand new car and she sold it. Clothes, jewelry, you name it, we bought it and it was never enough for her."

"I'm sorry."

Bill nodded. "Thank you for understanding."

"No. I'm sorry you're not smart enough to realize all she wanted was to be accepted for who she is. You didn't want the same life as your father, so you left. Why can't you see it's the same for her? She doesn't condemn you for having the life you do; she just wants a different one for herself."

Drake turned to leave. He was getting into his truck when Bill emerged from the hotel.

"Hey," Bill called, waving at Drake.

Drake stopped and faced him. "Yeah?"

"Do you really think she'd want us at the wedding?"

"Yeah, probably. Especially if you can act like you're happy for her and you're okay with her decisions. If you can't do those things, then don't bother." He got in his truck but before he closed the door he spoke in a threatening manner. "If you are there and you do anything to ruin her happiness, I will throw your ass in the harbor. Same goes for your wife and that guy you brought with you."

"Fair enough. When is it going to be?"

"Tuesday on *The KayLeigh*. Two in the afternoon."

"She's getting married on a boat?"

"Yeah, and I better not hear a single comment about it." He slammed his door, and pulled away from the hotel.

Chapter Twelve

Shawn stood in Cap's stateroom, twisting her hands together. Kirima, Celia and Patricia chattered as they fussed with her hair and flowers. After she'd stood the coddling as long as she could, Shawn backed away from them. "I have to go," she said.

"What? Where?" Kirima asked in a panic.

"I need to see Drake." Shawn turned toward the door.

Patricia moved in front of her. "You can't see him. It's bad luck."

Shawn met Patricia's gaze. "Patricia, we're getting along and I think I'm even to the point where I like you. But I guarantee if you don't move, I'll move you and we probably will never be friends. Right now, I want to see Drake." She waited a moment to let Patricia decide. After a few seconds, Patricia stepped aside.

"Thank you," Shawn walked from the room, through the galley and down the hall into the bunkroom.

"Shawn, what are you doing here?" JP asked, and tried to block her from Drake.

"I want to see Drake," she said.

"Why?" JP asked.

"It doesn't matter why."

"I can't let you do that."

Shawn clenched her fist. "You know how you think it's funny I punched Drake when I first met him?" she asked.

JP chuckled. "Yeah, it's a great story. I wish I'd seen

it."

Shawn narrowed her eyes. "If you don't get out of my way, you're going to see it from Drake's perspective."

JP's smile faded and he stepped to the side.

Shawn smiled when she saw Drake.

He moved toward her and took her hands. "You're absolutely beautiful."

"You are, too."

"What's up?" Drake asked in concern.

"I missed you." She kissed his cheek. "And I didn't want them to keep fussing over me. I don't like it."

"I understand."

"Maybe you've noticed I'm not much for tradition, so how about we have some champagne before the ceremony," Shawn suggested.

"Why? Do you have to be drunk to marry me?"

Shawn kissed him again. "I need a drink to keep me from rumpling your tux. Where did you find a tux in this town on such short notice, anyway?"

Drake laughed. "A man never reveals his sources."

"What if I hadn't found a wedding dress? You'd look a little silly if I showed up in jeans and a fishy-smelling sweatshirt."

"It's a chance I was willing to take. Besides, Celia told JP you'd bought a dress."

Shawn took him by the hand and led him into the galley to pour a glass of champagne. She sipped from it and offered it to Drake.

He took a couple swallows and handed it back. "There's beer in the fridge."

"Good." She dumped the champagne from the glass down the sink drain and refilled the flute with beer. They laughed and were finishing the shared glass of beer when Shawn's parents walked into the galley.

Shawn's mouth gaped. "What are you doing here?"

"We wanted to be here for your wedding," Bill said and hugged Shawn awkwardly and shook Drake's hand. "It looks like we're too late, though. Congratulations."

"You're not too late. We decided to have a toast

before the ceremony." She smiled. "You know me. I can't do anything the way I'm supposed to."

Drake laughed. "That must be why I love you."

Deb stepped forward and kissed Shawn's cheek. "You look beautiful, dear." She kissed Drake's cheek as well, and said, "Thank you for inviting us."

Shawn looked at Drake. "You invited them?"

"I figured you'd want your dad to walk you down the aisle, even if you are too stubborn to ask him yourself."

Shawn felt tears well up in her eyes and she whispered, "I love you so much."

"I love you, too. Now, dry up and I'll see if I can round up the crew." Drake kissed Shawn, squeezed her hand, and left the galley.

Shawn looked at her parents. "I thought you left."

"No, Drake stopped us." Bill cleared his throat. "He's a good man. You're lucky to have him and he's lucky to have you."

Shawn nodded in agreement and wrapped an arm around the waist of each of her parents. She looked up as Celia and Kirima walked into the galley.

"Ready?" Celia asked.

Shawn turned to her parents. "Are you guys ready to walk me down the aisle?"

"It's supposed to be the father of the bride," Shawn's mother said as she stepped back.

Shawn held out her hand to her mom.

"Oh, what the heck. You're only getting married once. You might as well do what you want," Deb said.

"Exactly."

JP offered his arms to Celia and Kirima. The three walked out of the galley and toward the deck where Drake, Cap and Patricia were waiting with the judge who was performing the ceremony.

Shawn paused as her parents started forward. They turned to look at her.

"I love you guys. You know that, right?"

The three hugged, and when Shawn's parents stepped back, Deb whispered, "You too, baby."

Bill patted Shawn's hand and they walked down the aisle.

When they reached Drake, Bill shook his hand. "Thank you for making my daughter happy and welcome to our family, for what it's worth."

"Thank you for making her happy."

Deb reached up, hugged Drake and kissed him on the cheek. "Bless you."

Drake kissed her back, released her and reached for Shawn.

With a smile, she kissed him. When she pulled away, she said, loud enough for everyone to hear, "Don't worry. You can kiss me again when we're done with the ceremony."

The End

About the Author

Lana Voynich has been writing stories for as long as she can remember. A love of books was instilled early by her parents, and when she ran out of reading material in her childhood home, she started making up her own stories. Once she even wrote a story about a frog on the back of a tissue box while trapped in the car on a family road trip.

Lana often wonders what happens to the people in her dreams when she wakes, so she writes their stories to satisfy her curiosity. When not reading or writing, Lana enjoys knitting socks, genealogy research, kayaking, snowmobiling and spending time with her family.

Visit Lana's website at www.lanavoynich.com.